QUICKENING

CERES

KEVIN MICUCH

CHARLESTON, AR:

COBB PUBLISHING

2019

Cover artwork by Dwayne Stacho

Published in the United States of America by:
Cobb Publishing
704 E. Main St.
Charleston, AR 72933
CobbPublishing@gmail.com
www.CobbPublishing.com

ISBN:
978-1-947622-25-8

CHAPTER 1

He reached out his hand, quiet as possible to avoid detection, and inhaled the sweet aroma of the fresh bread he was about to steal. He shoved it swiftly under his coat and breathed a sigh of relief. No one saw.

"Hey! Stop that punk!"

So much for that, Nevek thought. His heart pounded rapidly in his chest as he took off as fast as his feet would permit. He glanced upward at the sun, slowly sinking on the horizon. Darkness crept over the market as the sol came to a close. His hands perspired, and his heart rate accelerated even more. He looked back at the angry market owner chasing him. *Time to put it into second gear.* Nevek tried dodging a fruit stand, but clipped his foot on it. He winced in pain as he landed on his arm, but quickly regained his balance.

"Get back here!"

"How did he see me?" Nevek said to himself, as he sprinted down a corner road. The owner was surprisingly fast, but Nevek was a little faster. He turned down another side street and skidded behind a hover car. He peeked underneath the car, his silver, spiked hair almost touching the cold pavement. He saw the owner arguing with an elderly lady who had gotten in his way, causing him to lose track of his prey. With one last outburst of anger, the owner shouted, "You little schmuck! If I ever catch you, I'm gonna break your legs!"

"Yeah, you wish," Nevek said under his breath, trying to downplay how narrow the escape actually was.

He didn't steal that often. Only when necessary to help out his old man. Besides, everybody would steal some bread to feed their ill father, right?

Nevek stepped up the walkway. He looked into the night sky as a shooting star flew across. He pulled the loaf of bread from his coat. It got a little squished in all the excitement, but he didn't mind.

"Dad, I'm here," he shouted after he walked in the door.

"In here," his father shouted from the kitchen.

"I got you some bread. Not the one you wanted. It's the one you said is just *okay*. How you feeling today?" Nevek put the bread on the counter and turned to see his father's bleak countenance. He looked like he'd been crying. The clasping of the oxygen pump was the only response. "What's wrong, Dad?" Nevek said as he ripped off a piece of bread and stuck it in his mouth.

His father stared at the stars outside from his favorite chair. He finally looked at his son. "I had my last appointment today."

Confusion spread across Nevek's face. "What do you mean *last*?"

"I'm not going to any more doctors. Not taking any more shots. No more medication."

Nevek walked around the table and sat down across from his father. "What? Where is this coming from?"

"The doctor said that nothing is helping my condition. None of it is helping my body improve. So, I decided to just stop everything."

"So, you're just giving up?" Nevek's annoyance was clear in his voice.

"Nev, no, I'm still gonna enjoy my time," his father said with a chuckle. "I'm just going to see where life takes me."

"I can't believe with the technology we have, we still don't have a cure for this. What about those pills you were taking? Those helped, right?"

"For a little bit but my body got used to them. So after a while, they had no effect."

"I'm so sorry dad," Nevek said as he got up to give his father a hug.

"Don't be, Nevek. We'll just see where this thing goes. Now head on home and get some rest. Don't you have an exam coming up?"

"Yes sir. Maybe I'll go study instead. I'll try to not stay up too late," Nevek said as they pulled away from each other. His dad's body might be failing but his mind was still there—and it was one of the best.

Looking back at his dad, Nevek started to get choked up. *I can't cry,* he thought. *He needs me to be strong.*

They said their goodbyes and Nevek walked down the street to the CUET. The Ceres Underground Electric Tram was the cheapest way to get around on Ceres. It was the most utilized mode of transportation, unless you were wealthy enough to own a hover car. (Of course, walking was always a good option too.) There were CUET stations in each of the five cities on the planet so people could get anywhere with relative ease.

Nevek attended Lessur Academy, which was more than

a half-hour away in Napia, so he took the tram between there and his dad's house. The school in Valtux was closer, but his dad didn't think too highly of it.

The CUET came to a halt, and the door opened to an empty tram. Nevek needed the solitude. Tears filled his eyes and ran down his cheeks as he tried to deal with the news. He and his dad had just recently grown closer. He was a troubled kid but his father had continually encouraged him through his adolescent years. Now in college, Nevek was beginning to turn his life around, and his father was the reason for it.

Nevek's mother had left the family two years earlier. His father raised him and his older sister, Arys, on his own for a while. Eventually, they got older and Arys left for school, so it was just the two of them. They had their ups and downs as any father and son would. Probably more downs, though, because of Nevek, but they always found a way to work things out. Nevek's father loved his kids and just wanted them to be happy.

The chime sounded as students began to pile in. The college and high school students shared a building, like the grade and junior high did. Those who graduated from high school had the option to take college courses to further their education. Nevek wasn't sure what he wanted to do with his life at this point, but he enjoyed learning, so he decided to take a couple of extra college courses to see what would transpire.

Someone jumped on Nevek's back, and he lost his balance. They both hit the ground with a loud thud.

"I'm so sorry man," Zavier held back a laugh as he

picked his friend up off the floor.

"You gotta stop doing that!" Nevek snapped with a bit of fire in his words.

"Woah, what's got you jumpy?"

"I don't wanna talk about it." Nevek turned and started to walk away. Zavier grabbed his shoulder and spun him around.

"Hey. C'mon man. It's me. You and I talk about every-thing." Zavier was right. There wasn't much the two hadn't discussed since they became friends back in high school. Nevek looked up to Zavier. Not literally, as Zavier was a few inches shorter, but because he was a little older. Zavier may have been held back a grade, but he had nearly a year of life experience on Nevek.

Nevek sighed. "My dad is stopping his treatments. I don't know how much time he has left."

"Oh, I'm so sorry to hear that Nev." The two embraced in a small hug.

"I gotta get to class," Nevek stated.

"Yeah me too. We'll grab a drink tonight. We'll talk more then," Zavier shouted as they headed in opposite directions.

Nevek reached his desk as the professor started giving out the instructions for the exam, but his mind was else-where. All he could think about was his father. *How much time does he have? Why is he just giving up? Is there a cure that doctors don't know about yet? Would he even want a cure?*

Nevek came back to reality as the professor dropped a remote on the desk. After apologizing, he instructed the class to get out their slates as he projected the exam onto the wall.

Nevek stepped off the CUET and walked toward his father's house. He hadn't gotten the 'A' that he had hoped for, but with everything going on, he was pleased with the 'B-,' especially considering he didn't study for it.

As he neared the house, he noticed a hover car outside. *Don't recognize that one. Maybe Dad has a new friend.* Nevek walked in the always-unlocked door like normal. "Dad?" Nevek shouted.

"We're in here," his father yelled from the back room.

"Just wanted to tell you about my exam."

Nevek saw a woman sitting on the old, glass couch across the room—his mother, Lyneth. The woman who walked out on the family three years ago. The woman who betrayed her husband by leaving him for another man. He froze for a moment as they made eye contact. Her hair had gotten grayer since the last time he saw her.

"Hi Nevek," she said with a soft voice.

"What is she doing here?" Nevek fumed as he turned to his father, sitting in his recliner.

"You're not gonna say hi to your mother?" she inquired.

"Shut up! You have no right being here!" Two years of anger erupted out from his mouth.

"I beg your pardon?"

Her ex-husband butted in, "Nevek, don't talk to your mother like that."

"Are you serious, Dad?" Nevek turned back to his mother. "Get out! Get out now, and don't come back!"

"I have every right to be here, Nev. This was my house,

too."

"Yeah. *Was* you house. And don't call me that," Nevek began pointing at his mother

"Calm down, son. I called her over here," his father chimed in.

"Why would you do that?"

"Because she's a doctor."

"Well, I'm only a nurse," Lyneth noted.

"What does that got to do with it?" In the heat of the moment, Nevek didn't notice the obvious in the situation.

She stood up. "Honey, your father is ill. He just needed someone to talk to."

"You're the last person I thought he'd talk to," Nevek snarled

"Excuse me? I don't like your tone."

"Really? What are you gonna do? Ground me?"

"Look, I'm sorry if I'm a little concerned for your father."

"Hmm. That's not what you were saying when you walked out on us!"

Lyneth was taken back by the comment, at a loss for words. Nevek's father stepped in. "All right. Everybody calm down. Nev, it doesn't matter what she does. She is still your mother and you're gonna respect that. She has just been giving me some medical advice."

"Wait. Is that the reason you've stopped taking your meds? Because she told you to! I don't believe this. I'm out of here!" Nevek headed towards the door. "Oh, and got a B- on my exam today," he yelled as he left.

Lyneth glared at her ex-husband. "You're unbelievable! He doesn't know, does he?"

"No, he doesn't," he sighed

"I cannot believe you let him think that about me. He thinks *you're* the victim here! This is exactly why I left you!" she said as she stormed out too.

Zavier hocked a loogy as the two friends entered Sprokutt's in the southern end of Napia. It was the taproom they went to get away from their problems.

They sat at a booth near the back. Zavier looked around for the nearest server before finally noticing the agitated look on Nevek's face. "Yo. What's with you?"

"My mom."

Zavier looked confused. "Yeah… You haven't seen her in like two years. What about her?"

"No, she's here. Her and my dad have been talking apparently."

"You mean like getting back together?"

"No. They've just… been talking… I guess." Nevek shrugged his shoulders

"Oh. Do you know about what?"

"No. I couldn't bear to ask. I couldn't even look at her after what she's done. I walked out. Do you know what it's like growing up without a mother?" Nevek asked rhetorically

"Not really, no. It was my father that walked out on my mom, remember? We're like opposites," Zavier chuckled.

"Maybe that's why we get along so well," Nevek remarked as he chuckled too.

"Do you think…?" Zavier started before being interrupted by the server.

"Hi, I'm sorry about your wait."

"You calling me fat?" Zavier joked

"What? No. That's not what I meant." The young lady seemed embarrassed. Zavier apologized and the two ordered their usual meal and drinks. Nevek knew the drinks would ease his mind. It was a lot to take in.

After the meal and a few drinks, the conversation picked up again. "So, what do you think your mom wants?" Zavier asked as he leaned back in his seat.

"Ya know, I don't know."

"Maybe she has the cure for your dad," Zavier joked with a snicker.

Nevek's face quickly became serious. "Ya think?" Thoughts began racing through his head. He was a little buzzed from the alcohol, so his mind was all over the place. *Does she really have a cure? Or at least know something about his father?* Whatever it was, he was determined to get to the bottom of it. Nevek looked up at his friend. "I'm gonna find out what's going on. If she has the cure, I'm gonna get it from her." He slammed his fist on the table, got up from the booth, and headed out.

"It's okay!" Zavier shouted. "I got the bill! Don't worry about it."

Nevek started down the street. The CUET station was just a few blocks away. As he walked, he looked up at another shooting star. He had seen plenty of them in his lifetime, enjoying watching them until they were out of his line of vision. This one had a pretty long tail coming off the back of it, which he found a bit odd. *Okay, I must be drunk because that star looks like it's coming at me.* He stopped in his tracks and watched it get closer and closer. He was in awe. He couldn't look away. And then…

9

CRASH!

CHAPTER 2

The people of Ceres weren't surprised when foreign objects, such as meteors, crashed into their planet. Ceres is a dwarf planet orbiting just outside the Asteroid Belt, so things slam into it on occasion. This frightened many at first, but almost fifteen Cerean years in, people have gotten used to it. Most of the objects never did much damage any-way, so all people felt were minor tremors.

Initially, Nevek didn't think too much of it, but a glimpse of whatever it was that zipped by him told him this wasn't an asteroid. He couldn't tell exactly what it was from that split second though, so he decided to go check it out.

As he approached the unidentified object, dust settled around it and thick smoke was coming up from it. A small fire near the rear of it caused Nevek to keep his distance. The frame was pretty damaged from the impact. A big rock had sliced open the left side. He could barely make out wording. Still feeling a little buzzed, he started to head back. *How weird.* He took two steps and heard a *bang* and turned backed to the wreckage. *Is someone in there?*

As soon as he thought those words, another loud noise came from the other side of the metal object. To his surprise, someone kicked a door open and a figure fell to the ground. Nevek soon realized he wasn't hallucinating and rushed over to help the groaning person.

"Are you okay?" he asked.

As he got closer, he saw the person was a young woman. She looked to be around his age, but it was hard to tell with the cuts on her face and blood trickling down from her injuries. In the firelight, he saw she had a little darker skin tone than him, and had dark red hair. Probably because of the blood. *What was this girl doing?* Holding her side, she grunted, "Yeah."

"Here. Let me help," insisted Nevek. He began to get her out from the wreckage that used to be her ship. Sparks were flying off the front, which had caved in from the impact. With her arm over Nevek's shoulder, they both got to their feet and walked a few yards before a spark hit a leaking gasoline tank, causing a minor explosion. The woman fell forward to the ground, screaming in pain as she took Nevek down with her. He shielded his face from the brightness of the fire, then looked over at the woman lying next to him. "C'mon. We've gotta get to a hospital," he said. "What's your name?"

"Jerika Teverson," she softly replied, still holding her midsection. It took a lot for her to talk.

Two names? Nevek thought to himself. *That's odd.*

"Well, I'm Nevek. I'm gonna get you outta here."

"Thank you," she replied as she struggled to get back on her feet.

As they approached the road, they saw a couple walking in their direction. The man noticed them first. "We heard an explosion. Is everything all right?"

"Not really. She needs to get to a hospital," Nevek answered as the couple drew near.

The woman relieved Nevek as Jerika's aid. "I'm a nurse at the hospital in Zand. We'll take her there."

"Thanks." Nevek thought for a second, "Isn't Valtux closer though?"

As they guided Jerika to their hover car, the man looked back at Nevek and assured him, "My wife is more familiar with the doctors at her hospital. Don't worry. Your friend is in good hands."

Friend? I don't even know who the chick is, Nevek thought as he snickered to himself. "I do hope she is okay though," he said to himself.

"Is there anyone else?" the man shouted from the car.

"No, she's the only one," Nevek loudly replied. He looked back at the wreck. *Or was she? I'd better go back and see.*

He turned and watched the couple drive off. "I guess it didn't matter now," he thought as he jogged back toward the wreckage. He got as close as he could when something on the ground caught his eye. *Maybe Jerika dropped it.* Thinking she might want it, he picked it up and put it in his pocket.

It was late and fatigue crept up on him. He saw no other signs of life, so he decided to call it a night and headed back to his dorm.

As he boarded the CUET, he noticed he wasn't alone. He just sat up front, not wanting to walk to the back anyway. The thought of Jerika kept popping into his head. *Who is she? Where is she from? What was she doing out there?*

The CUET reached the Nevek's station, and he got off the tram. He made his way up to his dorm room, tiredness overtaking him. *What a day. First, your mother comes back into town and you don't know what she wants. Then a strange girl comes crashing into your life.* Nevek chuckled

13

a little at the day's events.

He slipped his shoes off as he entered his dorm room. He took his coat off and tossed it over the chair next to him. As it hit, Jerika's device smacked the floor. He picked it up and set it on his desk.

His face hit the pillow as he slammed into bed. He turned onto his back and closed his eyes. *What is that on the desk?* He couldn't get the question out of his head, but was too tired to get up. *Is it important? Does she even need it?* His curiosity won the battle and he rolled back out of bed.

He picked up the faded yellow machine. It resembled his slate, his handheld computer, but an earlier model, like it had been out-dated for a long time. It was a little heavier than his slate too. He searched to see how it turned on. *There's gotta be a power button somewhere.* After a few moments of searching, he pressed what looked like a button on the back, which booted it up. The screen was a little scratched from the accident, but all in all, it still looked to be good condition. The initial load screen showed a cross for a few seconds, but then it displayed some text. There were just the words "One Timothy" on it. He started to scroll down with his finger and something caught his eye. Jerika had highlighted a sentence. *"For this is good and acceptable in the sight of God our Savior, who desires all men to be saved and to come to the knowledge of the truth."*

What does that mean? Saved from what? What truth? He shook his head in disappointment and regretted getting out of bed. He turned off the device and tossed it back on his desk. He laid back down and wondered what kind of dreams he was going to have as he dozed off.

The ring of his telecom awoke Nevek from his slumber. Still half asleep, he answered it.

"Hey man! What's cookin'?" Zavier said from the other end.

"Nothin' much." Nevek yawned as he sat up in bed and started rubbing his eyes.

"You okay? You left in kind of a hurry last night."

"Yeah. I just have a lot on my mind right now. Sorry about that. I'll get you back next time."

"Yeah, you owe me. Things got a little weird last night after you left. I almost had to knock this dude out."

"Really? Sorry I missed it," Nevek joked. Zavier liked to embellish a bit.

"Yeah right! You would have been running the other way like a girl."

"We both know I would have had to help you off the floor, Zav." Nevek chuckled.

Zavier got quiet before muttering, "whatever."

"Well I had a crazy night too. I met this girl," Nevek paused. "Sort of."

"Woah! Really? Was she hot? I bet she wasn't. You seem to get the ugly ones." Zavier laughed

"You know, I couldn't really tell. She was too messed up."

"I knew it!" Zavier exclaimed "The ugly ones always flock to you." Zavier began laughing again.

Nevek sighed. "You're unbelievable man. No. She just fell from the sky. I kinda helped her out. She was in bad shape."

"Are you playin' me?"

"No, I'm serious. Her name is Jerika Teverson."

"What? Two names?" Zavier questioned.

"Yeah, I thought that was weird too… Maybe she was drunk," Nevek joked.

"Man, that's crazy. You need to stay far away from her."

"Yeah. Maybe." Nevek's telecom began ringing again, notifying him of another call. He got confused when he saw a number he didn't recognize. "Hey Zav, let me call you back." Before Zavier could respond, he hung up to take the other call. "Hello?"

"Nevek, it's your mother. I just wanted to tell you that I'm taking your father to the hospital."

Nevek got out of bed. "What's wrong? Is he okay?"

"He's just having some complications. Nothing to worry about. I just wanted to inform you."

Nevek didn't trust her, and was certain she was up to something. "I'll be right down," he said as he ended the call, not giving his mother a chance to say anything else. He put on some clothes and headed out the door. He had time before class started anyway.

The doctors treating Nevek's father were at the hospital in Zand, in the southern region of the planet. The specialists that dealt with more serious diseases worked primarily at this location. It wasn't close, but Nevek didn't care. He didn't want his mother taking care of his father. Even if it was just a short visit, he needed to know what was going on. He had only gone to a few of his father's appointments, but now he felt he should be at all of them. The CUET pulled up just as he got to the stop.

Nevek disembarked the CUET as the sun was starting to set. His anxiety grew as he approached the hospital doors. *I hope he's not dying. Not now. I'm not ready for that.*

He made his way to the front desk. The receptionist was a typical elderly woman, probably a former nurse that just knew her way around the hospital. Her name tag was turned around so Nevek couldn't address her properly. He gave her his father's name and she gave him the room number. Saying a quick "thanks," he went through the double doors. As he walked down the hallway, he saw Lyneth standing outside the room. *Well that's convenient.* He was glad he didn't have to go search for the room. Lyneth looked up at him as he came closer.

"I told you, you didn't have to come down here," she said softly.

Nevek didn't care. His focus was on his father. "Tell me what happened," he exclaimed, concerned.

"Everything is fine. His oxygen tank malfunctioned so he was having trouble breathing," she said trying to calm her son.

"You couldn't fix it?"

Lyneth sighed. "I'm only a nurse. I don't know how those things work."

"But, he's okay though?" he asked trying to look into the room.

Lyneth smiled, trying to remain cordial. "Yes. Everything is fine. He's just resting now." She saw her son was relieved by the news. "I can see you really love your father. It's good to see that you're involved in his life."

"Well, yeah. He raised me. Molded me into who I am today." Lyneth leaned in to give him a hug, but Nevek backed away with his hands in the air. "So, what are you doing here?"

"He wanted me to drive him here."

"So, you were with dad again?"

"Yes, Nevek. We've reconciled our relationship. We're civil now. And I think *we*," she gestured toward him, "should do the same."

"Why? What if I don't want to? You left us, remember?" Nevek became agitated and started to feel uncomfortable.

"Nevek, I'm your mother. I want us to have a relationship again."

"Sorry, I just think it's too soon." Nevek backed up. He looked away and saw a sign on the wall that read 'Zand Hospital.' *Oh, snap. This is the hospital where that couple brought Jerika.* His eyes widened as he looked back at his mother. "Mom, I gotta go." He squeaked with each step as he walked down the clean hallway.

A smile crept onto Lyneth's face as she watched her son go through the doors. "At least he called me 'mom'."

A nurse, carrying a chart, walked past Nevek and approached Lyneth. She looked at the chart and asked, "Is this your husband?"

"Ex-husband, yes," she corrected.

"It appears he's got an infection on his lungs that we didn't see before."

Lyneth's voice began to tremble. "Is he going to be all right?"

"We gotta run a test to see what it is. He should be able to just take some medication for it though. Just wait out here please," the nurse directed.

Lyneth looked back at the doors, hoping to see her son walking back through, but the doors remained closed.

Nevek made his way back up to the front desk. The same elderly woman was sitting there, looking down at a slate with some food next to it. "Excuse me," he said. "Is there a Jerika here?"

Without even looking up she searched through her slate. "Sorry, no one works here by that name."

"Oh... no I'm sorry. I was asking about a patient. Her name is Jerika Teverson."

"Oh, yes. The girl with two names," she said as she looked up at him. "A little strange, don't you think?" Nevek just smiled and nodded. She scrolled through her slate again, picking up some food and placing it neatly into her mouth. "Okay, she's in room 209. Just head up to the second floor and it will be at the end of the hall." Nevek thanked the woman and started to walk off. "Looks like she just got out of surgery about an hour ago."

"Okay, thank you." Nevek walked over to the elevator. On his way, he saw a cart of snacks. He hadn't eaten, so he snagged a couple of bags and consumed them as he entered the elevator.

A nurse walked out of Jerika's room. Nevek opened the door and saw her laying in bed, sleeping. She looked different without blood all over her. A flashback of the horrific scene appeared to Nevek as he examined her. He stepped near her bed, and saw her dark, burgundy hair. There was an IV in her left hand and a cloth bandage over her right temple, covering the gash she received from the crash. The only sound was the beeping of her monitor. He almost didn't want to wake her.

"Jerika?" Nevek said quietly. He didn't know for certain if she was asleep. He waited a few seconds with no response. He tried again, a little louder his time. "Jerika."

Jerika inhaled deeply, awakening from sleep. She opened her eyes for a second but quickly shut them due to the light. She put her arm up to shield her face. The effects of the anesthesia left her confused.

"Hey," Nevek said as he dimmed the lights.

As her sight started to come back, she lowered her arm and scanned the room. "Where am I?"

"Don't worry. You're in the hospital," Nevek said calmly.

Jerika turned to focus on where the voice was coming from. "Oh. And who are you?"

"I'm Nevek. I brought you here after your crash." He paused for a second. "Well...maybe not me *per se*, but I found you and a lovely couple brought you in here."

Jerika sat up. "Oh, yeah. I'm starting to remember now."

"I just stopped by to see how are you feeling?"

"Sore. But I'm thankful to be alive." She turned her head skyward. "Thank you."

"You're welcome?" Nevek glanced around the room to see if anyone else was in there.

Jerika let out a chuckle. "Not you. Well...thank you too. But I was thanking Jesus," she said as she pointed upward.

"Jesus?" Nevek raised his eyebrows. He looked at her as if she had something on her face. "Who's Jesus?" he questioned as he pointed to the ceiling.

"He's the Son of God." It was Jerika's turn to look at Nevek funny. "You don't know about Jesus?"

"Nope. Sorry. It doesn't ring a bell." He said as he shrugged his shoulders. "Should I have heard of him?"

Jerika was now embarrassed. "No, it's fine. I just thanked him for keeping me alive."

"Wow, you really are crazy. I think I'll get your nurse to come check on you." Nevek walked over to the monitor and pushed the button to alert the nurse. He started to walk back but something caught his eye. He looked back at the monitor and was dumbfounded. He couldn't believe what he was seeing. "There's no way," he thought. "It couldn't be." It had to be a mistake.

According to the chart, Jerika's nurse's name was Arys.

CHAPTER 3

Arys came up to the kitchen table. She nudged her little brother, making him spill his juice. "Hey!" he shouted. "Dad!"

"Arys, stop picking on your brother," her father begged.

"Where's the fun in that?" she asked rhetorically. Her father sighed.

"Why do you have to leave?" Nevek asked.

"Aw. Is my baby brother gonna miss me?"

"No!" he shouted childishly. "Well...maybe a little."

"I gotta start my life, kiddo." Arys messed up Nevek's hair. "I'm just going to Oxator to get my degree."

"Will you visit?"

"Sure I will."

"Okay, you better," the young Nevek yelled as he watched her walk out the front door. He bowed his head in sadness.

Nevek's father looked over at him. "Don't worry, Nev. She's just making her path. Just like you will one day."

Nevek snapped out of his daydream when he heard his name called. "Nevek, is that you?" Arys stood in the doorway in almost as much shock as her brother.

Nevek hadn't seen his sister since that day she left for school. She had gotten shorter. Or maybe Nevek had gotten taller. Her black hair was in a small ponytail. It looked shorter than the last time he saw her.

"Wow, it is you!" Arys ran over to her brother and embraced him. Nevek's arms went up automatically as he hugged her back. "What are you doing here?"

Nevek was at a loss for words. His mouth moved, but nothing came out.

"Are you okay, kiddo?" Arys asked as she pulled away.

"Yeah…it's just…good to see you," Nevek finally uttered.

"You too. It's been a long time. How have you been?"

"I'm doing well. I thought I'd never see you again."

"Oh, don't say that. You're gonna make me cry. What are you doing here?"

"I'm just checking up on my friend Jerika here."

Arys had forgotten she had a patient in the room. She looked over at Jerika waving at her. "Oh, I am so sorry!" she exclaimed as she walked over to check her patient.

"It's okay," Jerika replied. "I'm not the one who pushed the button anyway."

"Oh. Nevek, why'd you call for me?" Arys asked

Nevek walked over to them. "I don't know. She was talking crazy. I just assumed she was drugged up or something."

Arys gave a puzzling look towards her brother. "What do you mean?"

"I was telling him about Jesus," Jerika answered.

"What's Jesus?"

Jerika rolled her eyes. "Jesus is the Son of God. He saved me from my sins and he can save you from yours too."

Arys looked at her brother who shrugged his shoulders. She looked back at Jerika. "What do you mean? What sins?"

"Any sins you've committed. He can wash them away, if you let him. He can make you new."

"Wait, what are sins exactly?" Nevek inquired

"The wrongs you've done." Jerika realized she may have bitten off more than she could chew. How is it possible that they've never heard of God before? *This is worse than I imagined. Did I do the right thing in coming here?* She decided just to start from the beginning as she sat up.

"Okay. My name is Jerika Teverson. I come from a little town called Trinion on the planet Mars. Where I'm from, we are Christians. We believe in Elohim, our God, the creator of the universe, and his Son Jesus. From the very first man and woman he created, who were called Adam and Eve, man has done wrong in God's eyes. They have never been able to live up to his standards and have been separated from a relationship with him. So God devised a plan to have mankind united with him again in that he sent his son Jesus to die for our sins. Jesus then rose from the dead three days later. Now, with our acceptance of that sacrifice Jesus made, we can be freed from our sin and be in a relationship with God once again. We too, will be resurrected when we die so that we can live eternally with him in Heaven. I just wanted to come here to Ceres to tell others about this wonderful news." Jerika felt awkward when she saw the siblings blankly staring back at her. She didn't know what to say next.

After a brief silence, Nevek finally spoke. "Wow. I think you may have hit your head a little too hard when you crashed here. How much medication are you on?"

"None that I'm aware of."

"Yeah, I haven't given her anything yet," Arys declared.

Nevek looked up at the clock. "Well, that's quite an interesting story. I just don't really have time to hear anymore though. I'm gonna get going. It was nice meeting you." Nevek pointed at Jerika and headed for the door

"Okay, I'll walk you out," Arys said as she got up too.

Jerika leaned back in her bed and exhaled deeply. This was harder than she had thought. She had never gotten a response like that before. Usually, people were more open minded and accepting to the gospel of Jesus. At least back on her planet. Her mind went back to her overseers telling her not to go to Ceres. They warned her that it wouldn't be a wise decision. Being only converted a short time though, she had the passion of Jesus in her. She decided to work on her approach. This was a whole new world with a totally different mindset than she was used to. She just told herself to give it more time. God wouldn't let her down.

"Do you think Jerika's crazy?" Nevek asked Arys as they headed toward the front of the hospital.

"I don't know. That was a lot to take in. I just got assigned to her when I saw you guys. It was different, that's for sure."

"Yeah tell me about it. There is a god? This guy died in place of us? And this place 'Mars' sounds made up too. I mean, who does she think she's fooling?" They stepped outside into the frigid night. "Anyways, I've gotta get going. It was really nice seeing you, sis."

"You too, kiddo." The two embraced in a hug once more. "I'm so sorry I haven't seen you lately."

Nevek pulled away. "Don't be. I assumed you were

busy anyway."

"No, that's no excuse. When I get off tomorrow, we gotta catch up."

"I have class tomorrow, but yeah we do need to get together sometime. Now get back in there. It's cold out here." He chuckled. They exchanged telecom numbers and went their separate ways.

Nevek tried the best he could, but just couldn't concentrate in class. So many things had happened the past few sols. He couldn't quite process it all. *Why is mom here? What's going to happen to dad? How much longer does he have to live? Where has Arys been all this time? What was Jerika talking about?* Then something dawned on him. Arys worked at the same hospital that his dad was at. *I wonder if she knows he's there*, he thought.

"May I borrow your netbook?" The question startled him. He looked up from his blank netbook at Sqett, another student, looking back at him.

"What?"

"May I borrow your netbook to charge mine? It's about to die," Sqett explained.

"Yeah, sure," Nevek said as he handed his slate over. Nevek had almost a full battery so he didn't mind.

Sqett touched the two devices together for a few moments, then he handed Nevek's back.

"Thank you, sir," Sqett said as he turned back in his seat.

"You're welcome," Nevek smiled.

He looked over at Sqett as he listened to the teacher. Sqett was one of the smarter kids in class. His IQ was probably one of the best in the school. He always seemed happy too. Usually had a smile on his face.

The chime rang.

Nevek caught up with Sqett as they walked out of class. "Hey, man."

"Oh, hey. What can I do for you, Nevek?" Sqett asked, taken aback by Nevek talking to him. His timid personality didn't leand itself to much conversation with people.

"I got a question for you."

"Okay, sure."

"Well, we've only talked a few times in the past, but I know you're more intelligent than me, so I thought I'd ask you..." Nevek grew nervous.

"O...kay..."

"It's gonna sound crazy, I know, but do you believe there is a god?"

"A what?"

"You know, a god? Someone who created the planet we live on?" When he finished his question, he saw that Sqett was thinking.

"Well, I don't really see any evidence for there to be one. But this is a most intriguing inquiry. You have gotten my brain juices flowing. I will research it and return with an answer," Sqett said as he began to walk away. Nevek stopped him.

"You know what? Never mind. Forget I asked. It was a stupid question." Nevek walked away, feeling embarrassed. The smartest kid in the class didn't even know what he was talking about. "How dumb was I?" Nevek asked himself with a laugh.

Nevek got back to his dormitory as night was approaching. Fatigue was setting in as he sat on his bed. This truly had been a weird and tiring last few sols. He laid there, looking up at the ceiling. His eyes began to close when he remembered he still had Jerika's device. His curiosity again got the best of him.

He got out of bed and walked to the desk. He turned the device on and started scrolling through it. He came upon the eighth chapter of the story of someone named 'John'. Once again, Jerika had highlighted a passage. This time it was verses thirty-one and thirty-two. Nevek read the verses out loud, *"Then Jesus said to those Jews who believed him, 'If you abide in My word, you are My disciples indeed. And you shall know the truth, and the truth shall make you free'."*

That sounded like the last one he read about God wanting everyone to come to the knowledge of truth. This God must be the Elohim guy Jerika was talking about. What is this truth though? How does this truth set them free? And free from what? Whatever it was, Nevek just didn't understand.

He turned off the device and set it on the floor. He rolled onto his side and thought about his father. *I bet this doesn't have an answer for this disease,* he thought. He doubted it did. He decided that it wasn't going to be useful to him at all.

And he fell asleep.

CHAPTER 4

It was a busy night, so the taproom was noisy. Like most nights, it was full of people having a good time, enjoying each others company with a few drinks (some, too many drinks). It was no different for Nevek and Zavier. Two friends enjoying a good time. That's why they liked the taproom scene, and why they went there after classes were over. Nevek tried to enjoy his time, but couldn't, still thinking about everything that had happened. "Have you ever heard of Mars?" he randomly asked Zavier.

"Mars? No. I don't think so. Why do you ask?"

Nevek shook his head. "No reason." He took a sip of his drink.

"Weird," Zavier snickered. "Hey, how's your dad doing?"

"Good. Had a bit of a scare a few sols ago, but everything's okay now."

"Oh, that's good."

"Yeah. I've been meaning to do a little research on his condition but I've been getting sidetracked. Things are settling down now though."

"That's cool, man. I hope things work out for you. Your dad is a good man."

Zavier looked up over Nevek's shoulder and waved his hand. Nevek turned around to see an attractive woman walking towards them. His eyes widened as she brushed her blue hair off her neck with her hand and took a seat next to his friend.

"Hey babe," she said as she greeted Zavier with a kiss on the cheek.

"Hello beautiful," he replied. "I didn't know you were gonna be here tonight."

"Eh, plans fell through. But I knew you'd be up here, so I came up too." She looked over at Nevek sitting across from her. "Hi, I'm Endigo, but people just call me Endy," she said as she extended her hand.

Nevek shook her hand as Zavier finished the introduction: "This is my friend Nevek."

"Nice to meet you," Nevek replied

"Me and Nev go way back," Zavier explained.

"That's cool," Endy said. "So, have you guys tried the Fudge Monkey yet? It's a new drink they came out with." The boys shook their heads and agreed to try it. She got up from the table. "I'll go order us some."

Zavier watched her as she left the table. He had a smile on his face the whole time. He was still smiling when he noticed Nevek staring back at him. "What?"

"You didn't tell me you had a girlfriend," Nevek said, half-joking, half-serious.

"I didn't? I thought I did."

"No, I would have remembered something like that."

"Oh, my bad. Yeah we met a few sols ago. Oh, wait! I actually met her the last time we came here. When you left to meet up with your girl…Jessica…or something."

Nevek laughed. "Okay, first off, her name is Jerika. And second, I'm not *seeing her*. I actually don't know if I'll even see her again. I'm trying to stay focused on one thing right now and that's trying to find a cure for my dad."

"Okay, I got you."

"Oh, and you'll never guess who I saw at the hospital when I went."

"Who?"

"My sister, Arys. She was Jerika's nurse."

"You have a sister?"

Nevek sighed. "You're an idiot. Yes. I hadn't seen her in a long time. Ever since she went away for school."

Endy came back with three drinks and passed them out. "Okay. Try these."

"Actually, I gotta get going. It was nice meeting you Endy," Nevek said as he wiped his mouth and got up.

Zavier sighed as he slammed his hands on the table. "Seriously? Don't worry, I'll pay for this...again!" he yelled sarcastically.

Endy looked over at Zavier. "Can I have his drink?"

Nevek found himself in Napia where he walked into the cafetorium, a public place where anyone could go at any time and access the internet for research or study. There were only three cafetoriums on the planet. The other two were in Valtux and Elvers. He sat at one of the smart screens and began his search.

A quick search of his father's symptoms resulted in lists of various diseases, most of which he'd never heard of before. He scrolled through pages and pages without any luck. After a while, he came across one that looked promising. That's when his telecom went off. He looked down to see that Arys was calling him. His eyes grew as a he smiled. *My sister wants to talk to me!* He answered that call. "Hey, sis!"

"Hey, kiddo. Where ya at?" she asked.

"I'm at the cafetorium in Napia."

"Oh. What are you doing there?"

"A little research," he said as he continued reading what was on the screen.

"Oh, for school?"

"Uh…sure," Nevek lied.

"Well, you wanna hang out before I go into work?"

"Yeah, that'd be fine. I don't know how long I'll be here though." He stopped looking at the screen and focused on the call.

"Oh, don't worry about it. I'll come to you. I'm heading that way anyway."

"Oh, okay. I'll see you soon."

Nevek put his telecom down and turned back to the screen. He couldn't help but think about Arys. This, of course, led to thoughts about Jerika. He stopped to ponder. "Hmm. I wonder…" he said out loud. He typed in 'Mars' in the search engine.

Nothing came up.

"What?" he said, confused. "That's interesting."

Arys made her way into the crowded cafetorium. The smell of coffee pierced her nostrils. Being her first visit to this one, it took her a few minutes to find her brother. She walked past a group of guys in a booth as one of them finished a crude joke. She sighed as she left them behind. *I've heard that one before, it's not that funny.*

She finally located her brother near the back. Seeing he was deep in thought, she decided to sneak up on him. She crept up behind him and said his name in a really high-pitched voice as she gently touched him on the shoulder.

"Ahhh!" Nevek shrieked. He almost fell out of his chair as he turned to see Arys laughing.

"You're such a wimp," she said as she messed with his hair.

"And you're a jerk!" He swatted her hand away. "You can't mess with the spikes."

"Whatever."

Arys sat down next to Nevek and took a glimpse at his screen. "Whatcha reading?"

"I was looking up things about Mars and gods. Turns out, there's nothing. Zilch. I think our friend may be pulling one over on us."

"Hmm. That is interesting. I wonder why she'd be telling stories. What could she gain from it?"

"Beats me," Nevek said as he shrugged his shoulders. "But now that I know, I can focus on more important things."

"Oh, yeah? Like what?"

"Finding a cure for dad. I don't think he's gonna last much longer."

"What do you mean?"

Nevek looked puzzled. "You didn't know dad was sick?"

"No. I haven't seen him in a while, dingus!" She smacked Nevek's forehead. "He probably deserves it anyway."

"Hey! Don't say that about Dad! Mom was the one who left remember?"

"Yeah, but you know why she left, right?"

"Cuz she's a whore. That's why."

Arys laughed at his remark "No, dingus. Dad cheated

on her first. He's the whore."

Nevek was stunned into momentary silence. "Shut up. No he didn't." The words just came out. He looked back at his monitor.

"Yes, he did. After I left you guys, Mom and I bumped into each other one day, like we did, and she told me he was fooling around with his secretary. She said he claimed it was only twice, but it's hard to believe him. Did you really not know this?"

Nevek didn't know what to say. He stared at the floor in shock. *Why would he not tell me? How could he have done that?* The shock quickly turned into anger. He had to find out the truth. He pushed pass Arys and walked away.

"Hey! Where are you going?" Arys asked

Nevek turned around and started walking backwards. "To find out what's going on!"

He turned back around and stormed out.

CHAPTER 5

Nevek was quite nervous. His anger had died down during the ride over. He walked up to his childhood home, hoping what Arys said wasn't true. *She wouldn't lie to me, right? How could I not know this before?* It was time to face the facts. Nevek took a deep breath as he walked through the front door.

He stepped quietly, not wanting to startle his father. He peaked into the living room, but didn't see anyone. Noises coming from Arys' old bedroom—which had been turned into a den—caught Nevek's attention. He walked toward the sound of a television, and saw his dad sitting in his chair. "Hey, Dad," he said softly.

His father looked up at him standing in the doorway. "Hey, son. Come on in."

Nevek walked in and sat in the other chair. His father didn't look much different from the last time he saw him. Still weak and having trouble breathing. "How are you holdin' up?" He didn't know how to bring up the subject weighing on his mind.

"Well, good I guess." He scratched his chest. "This machine isn't very comfortable though."

"What machine?" Nevek asked.

His father lifted up his shirt, exposing a tiny device attached to his chest. They gave me this in the hospital. It monitors the disease. I was there for three sols. How come you didn't come up?"

"I actually did come up, but mom said you were resting

so I didn't wanna bother you. But then I ran into Arys."

"Oh really? What was wrong with her?"

Nevek was confused for a second. "What? No, she's a nurse there. I hadn't seen her in so long, I almost didn't recognize her."

His father smiled. "Well good for her. Following in her mother's footsteps I see."

"Yep." Nevek didn't want to get into small talk. He decided to just get it over with. "She also told me something disturbing."

"Oh yeah? What's that?"

"I didn't believe it at first but then..."

His father interrupted, "Nev, just spit it out."

Nevek was a bit surprised at his father's impatience. *The disease must be wearing on him.* He stroked his chin as he got to the hard part. "She told me the reason mom left us. She left because you cheated on her."

His father looked back at the television and sighed.

"So, is it true?"

His father's silence all but confirmed it, but Nevek had to hear it straight. "Dad, I gotta know..."

"Yes, it's true!" his father interrupted him again.

Nevek couldn't believe what he just heard. He clenched his fists and cursed as he shot up from his seat. "What is wrong with you, huh!? Why am I just now hearing about this!?" The words shot out his mouth like a cannon.

His father was a little surprised. "I just didn't think it was that important, I guess."

"Not important!? How could this not be important?"

His father shrugged with his hands up as high as they could go.

"I don't even know if I can look at you the same way again. You disgust me! And mom…how could you let me build up hatred towards her? She didn't deserve that."

"Hey, she's not that innocent either, you know. We're just even."

Nevek was appalled. "Even? EVEN!? No, she was just getting away from you! Just like I'm doing now. I'm outta here!" Nevek stormed to the front of the house and out the door.

He headed down the street, infuriated by his father's lack of remorse. He felt betrayed. He wasn't a child anymore. Why was he kept in the dark most of the time? He wasn't sure but he knew alcohol would put his mind at ease. He called up Zavier.

"Okay, I'll meet you at the taproom then," Zavier replied.

"No, I wanna try something different. Meet me at the one in Elvers."

"Okay, I'm with Endy though. You mind if she comes too?"

"The more the merrier."

Three drinks in and the trio was quite inebriated. Nevek didn't get drunk as often as Zavier and Endy, so it wasn't long before the alcohol's influence came out. He told the other two about the revelation he had been given earlier. Every time he thought about it, he took another drink. He was still in disbelief, but with every gulp, the feeling was pushed down for a few moments. Zavier and Endy were enjoying themselves, encouraging Nevek to just forget about life for a while. A couple of hours in, the three of them were plastered.

Nevek decided to head out, and the others agreed. He got up quickly and bumped into a man, causing him to spill his drink on both of them. "Hey! Watch where you're going, bud!" Nevek snapped, before looking up at a man a few inches taller and a lot more muscular. He had an unpleasant look on his face.

"Where I'm going? You, little punk, are the one that walked into me!" He pushed Nevek into the table he had been sitting at, knocking it over. Nevek stumbled over with it and onto the floor. He winced and was slow to get up. A small crowd started to form around them, intrigued at the commotion.

The muscular man was a little buzzed, but had no problem getting his point across. "Now listen here. I run this taproom and I ain't seen you or your friends before. I'll be kind and give you one chance to get out before trouble starts."

Zavier smiled when he saw a barkeeper come out from the back. As his friends apologized and headed for the door, Zavier walked up to the bar and spoke to the barkeeper. "Hey, that gentleman over there said that he'd get our tab. Nice guy. Thank you," he said and pointed to the brute Nevek had just encountered. The barkeeper looked a bit confused, but accepted the statement. Zavier patted him on the shoulder and left.

The three walked out and went their separate ways; Zavier and Endy one way and Nevek the other. Nevek staggered from side to side and his head started to hurt. He heard the taproom door swing open and a man cursing loudly. He turned around, but couldn't make out who it was, so he resumed walking.

The man, however, caught sight of Nevek almost immediatley. "Come back here you little punk!" he shouted as he started the pursuit.

Nevek turned his head and saw a big blurry figure gaining on him. He ran into an alley trying to lose it. His heart began to race as he found a dimly lit door nearby. He tried to open it, but it remained locked. Drunk and unable to see in the dark alley, Nevek tripped over his feet and hit his head on the wall. His head began to spin and he fell to the ground and rolled over onto his back. Just before his eyes closed, he saw a shadow of someone standing over him. Then everything went black.

Arys walked down the hallway of the hospital, heading back to Jerika's room. *What is she going to make up today?* She did find Jerika's stories entertaining though, and she enjoyed talking with her. With a tray of food for her patient in hand, she entered the pristine room.

Jerika heard the door open as she was waking from a nap. Sleeping inclined was uncomfortable due to soreness, but necessary. She enjoyed the fact that she didn't need to be hooked up to machines anymore. It made things a little easier. The sight of the food immediately made her stomach growl.

"Hey, Jerika. How do you feel?" Arys asked.

Jerika tried to stretch. "My sides are sore," she grunted

"Well, a couple of broken ribs will do that."

"Yeah. That's what the doctor said. I'm getting hungry too. I'll take whatever you have there." Jerika pulled the table near her bed.

"Sure. Not a problem," Arys said as she set the tray in front of Jerika.

Jerika bowed her head and closed her eyes for a couple of seconds. She then raised her head and returned to talking with Arys. "Hey, sorry about the other sol. Me talking about God and everything. I know it was a lot to take in. Especially when you've never heard of him before."

Arys smiled. "No, it's fine. I kinda liked the little story you gave."

Oh, it's not a story, it's the truth, Jerika thought. She didn't want to further complicate things though, so she just brushed it off and took another bite of food.

"It looks like you're doing okay. Do you need anything else?"

"No, thank you. I want to thank you for taking care of me," she said after she swallowed.

"Oh, you're very welcome. You're in the best hospital on the planet. And I'm not just saying that because I work here," Arys laughed at her own joke.

Jerika started to laugh but couldn't without inducing pain. "Oh, don't make me laugh. It hurts too much."

"Oh, sorry," Arys smiled apologetically.

"The hospitals on Mars are good too. Thankfully, I haven't had to be in them much. This is really my first serious injury."

Arys became a little uneasy when she heard Jerika talk about Mars again. She chose not to make things awkward though, and just play along to humor her. "Well, here we just want our patients to get better. Just keep getting rest."

"Yeah that's one thing I'm doing well here: resting. These beds are pretty comfortable," she said as she felt the mattress. "One thing though, I'm not used to this time change. I think I've been here a few sols already."

Arys was quite bemused at that statement, but she continued to play along. "Yeah. A sol here on Ceres is just over nine hours."

Jerika's jaw dropped. "Nine hours!? On Mars it's twenty-four and a half hours. Your planet spins fast!"

Arys was really confused now. She wasn't sure what to think. *That place doesn't really exist, does it?* "Yeah, that's a long time," she blurted out.

"Well, compared to here, yeah," Jerika said, excited to have learned something new about the planet. "Is your planet red too?" Jerika said trying to continue the interaction. She didn't get much seeing as she only knew a few people on Ceres.

"Actually, I should get going." Arys couldn't handle anymore. She didn't know why, but Jerika's questions were making her uncomfortable. "I do have other patients that need tending to," she said with a little nervous laughter.

Jerika was disappointed, but understood. "Okay, I'm all good here. Thank you."

Arys finished checking a few things and quickly walked out the door. After the door closed, she let out a big sigh. *Could Jerika really be from another planet?*

Are her stories true?

CHAPTER 6

Nevek's eyes hadn't yet adjusted when he realized his head was pounding. He felt like throwing up. It was a classic hangover. As the room slowly became clear, he saw the blue ceiling of his dormitory. He couldn't sit up for fear of falling off his bed, so he just let out a grunt.

"Oh good, you've awakened," he heard across the room.

Nevek looked over toward the voice. As his eyes focused, he saw Sqett walking in from the kitchen. "I did some research on the question you've inquired about and have found there aren't any gods."

Sqett's voice startled Nevek and his words confused him, but the immense headache overpowered his thoughts. The brightness of the lights didn't help matters either. "How did I get in my dorm? And how did you get in here?" Nevek finally uttered.

"The maintenance guy let me in. I got you up from the alley and brought you back here. You slept for a sol."

Nevek sat up slowly. "Ugh, my head." He cupped his hand over his head. "Have you been here the whole time?" he murmured.

"Yes. I wanted to inform you on the question you asked me. My search came up empty. I didn't find any evidence of any gods."

"Well, thank you, but you didn't have go through that."

"Oh, no. I thoroughly enjoyed the minute study. I just

couldn't find anything that suggests we're being watched. I mean, if they're out there, where are they? Why haven't we seen them?"

At that moment, a minor tremor shook the dorm room, caused by a small asteroid hitting the other side of the planet. The two braced themselves for a few seconds until it was over. It didn't help Nevek's hangover in the least. Jerika's device, among a few other things, fell to the floor. Sqett picked everything up for Nevek, but the device caught his attention. "What is this?" he inquired, showing Nevek.

"Um, not sure really. I met this girl who says she's from another planet." Sqett looked at Nevek as if he had two heads. "Yeah, that's the look I had too. She also believes that there's a god. I think that's the thing she uses to justify her claim."

"Really? What does it say?" he asked while examining the machine.

Nevek gradually became more alert as the effects of the hangover wore off. The wall supporting his every step, he slowly walked over and took the device from Sqett. "I haven't really read a whole lot of it. Just a few sections. It mentions 'truth' and it setting you free from something. I don't know. Didn't really think too much of it. I'll probably just give it back to her today."

Sqett looked a little confused. He pondered what Nevek had said. "Oh. This is why you asked me about a god. I understand now. Do you mind if I take a look at it?"

Nevek thought about it a bit. "Nah. It just seemed too farfetched. I'm gonna take it back."

"Well, let me see if I can figure out how to transfer the

files. I would like to take a gander at them."

"Uh, Okay." Nevek left his acquaintance for a moment to get ready to go visit Jerika.

Sqett inspected the device for a few seconds, trying to figure out how to copy the files. He was pretty tech savvy, more than most, but this one stumped him for a little bit. However, after a few moments, he finally got it to turn on. It looked different than what he was used to, but he was soon maneuvering around on it. He linked the device to his telecom and copied the files over. He shut the device off and set it back down on Nevek's desk. "So I'll see you in class," he shouted to Nevek.

Sqett's voice seemed a roar to Nevek's eardrums, still fighting his hangover. He grabbed his temples in pain. "Okay, yeah. See ya," he managed to mutter, shaking it off.

The door opened and Sqett headed out but stopped just when he heard Nevek say, "Hey." He turned around to listen.

"Thanks for bringing me back up here. That was nice of you. Sorry you had to see me like that." Nevek's embarrassment was evident in his tone.

"Oh no. Don't sweat it. I'm not sure I would have done it if it were anybody else, but I'm glad it was you so we could discuss the god thing."

Nevek smiled. "Gotcha. You know, we should hang out sometime. Get to know each other a little better."

That familiar smile slid across Sqett's face. "I would like that," he said, and walked out.

Nevek finished getting ready. He grabbed Jerika's device and headed out the door. As he walked to the CUET station, he tried to piece together the events that led him to being passed out. When he couldn't remember, he decided to call up Zavier. After a few seconds, he was greeted with a "Hey man!"

"Hey Zav."

"What's going on? Looking for another fun night?" Zavier started to laugh.

Nevek let out a chuckle of his own. "No. No. But funny you bring that up. I was gonna ask you about the other night. I don't remember much." Nevek had reached the station.

"Yeah, you can't hold your alcohol," Zavier jeered.

"Well, we went to that other taproom. That's about all I remember."

"Yeah, you almost got clobbered too. You got any bruises?"

Nevek was a little confused. "No, I'm good. That's crazy though. What did I do to deserve that?" The CUET had arrived and Nevek embarked. There were a few people onboard, so he took a seat in the back.

"You were toasted man. You went to get up from the table and crashed right into a guy that was way bigger then us. You ended up spilling a bunch of drinks on him." Zavier starting laughing again.

"Wow. Not cool. I'm never going back there again. That's for sure."

"Yeah, you were crazy. It probably didn't help that I gave him the bill too," Zavier chuckled.

Nevek was momentarily stunned by the statement. "What?"

"Yeah, I told the barkeeper to put it all on the guy's tab when we walked out. I didn't really get to see the guy's face when he found out though. Wish I did. He sounded pretty angry. We hightailed it outta there."

"Are you serious?" Nevek's tone got a little louder. "What is wrong with you!? You could have gotten me killed!"

Most of the people on the tram looked back in Nevek's direction and gave him dirty looks. He had forgotten for a moment that people could hear him.

"Woah! Chill out man. It was just a joke," Zavier said.

"Well, that's not funny. Friends don't do that type of stuff to each other." Nevek couldn't think of anything else to say. He ended the call with "I gotta go," and hung up on his friend.

He sat, a mix of anger and disappointment with Zavier. He didn't want Jerika to see him angry though, so he just let out one big punch to the back of the seat in front of him. That should do it.

The CUET stopped near the hospital in Zand and Nevek exited the station with a clear head. He wanted to put this part of his life behind him so he could focus on more important things. It was a busier night than usual and the waiting room was crowded. *Glad I'm not having to wait.* The doors opened and the stench of vomit pierced his nostrils as he saw a couple nurses cleaning up a recent mess. He covered his nose and mouth and turned away from the smell. In doing so, he bumped into another gentleman, causing Nevek to fall on his behind. The man lost his balance a little, but quickly regained it and let out under his breath, "Stupid kids." Nevek let out a little snicker as he got up while a few people stared at him. "My bad," he said to himself.

He started to walk to the reception desk, but finally remembered the room number Jerika was in and diverted back towards the hall. He arrived at the elevator and saw the table of candy again, this time noticing the prices. Nevek felt his empty pockets. Thinking no one would notice, he took one for a snack and boarded the elevator as he began to eat.

He followed the signs to the room, almost forgetting where it was. He got to the door and had a weird thought. *That would be pretty funny if she wasn't in this room anymore.* He smiled at the thought and opened the door. He saw Jerika watching television as he entered.

Jerika turned to the door. "Hey! I didn't know you were stopping by."

"Yeah," Nevek said. "Just figured I'd check in. See how you were doing."

"Actually, a lot better. Thank you." She turned the television off.

"Well, that's good to hear."

"Yeah, I should be ready to leave in a sol or two."

"Oh, really? That's also good to hear." Nevek sat down in a chair nearby. He had just met Jerika, but he was beginning to see her as an acquaintance—maybe even a friend. *Even if she is a little crazy. She is humble and easy to get along with.* And oddly enough, she did bring him and his sister back together again. That had to count for something. He figured getting to know her a little better was the least he could do. "So, how do you like Ceres?" he asked jokingly.

"Well, I haven't really seen a whole lot here," she

laughed.

"Yeah I know. I'm just messing around."

"I was telling your sister that I'm still adjusting to the sols here. They're much shorter than back home. You guys must have very strange sleep patterns with only nine hour sols. On Mars, they last around twenty-four and a half hours."

The information piqued Nevek's interest. He only knew of nine-hour sols. Naturally, he cocked his head and leaned in closer to inquire more. "Yeah, it's normal for us to be awake for a few sols at a time. And sometimes even sleep for a few," he explained. "Twenty-four hours though? Hmm, that's interesting. How long is a year?"

"Just about 687 sols."

Nevek was fascinated. "Wait, you came to a planet that has longer years? Why?"

"I told you. I came to spread the word of God." She sat for a moment, gathering her thoughts. "At least I thought I did. I don't know." At that moment, her eyes began to water. She turned away from Nevek.

"What's wrong, Jerika?" he asked. He felt bad. He didn't know what to do.

"It wasn't supposed to turn out like this," she answered, holding back tears. "I wanted to meet new people and tell them about Jesus. Since I've become a Christian, that's what I wanted to do. My mom would not be happy if she knew I was here."

"Your parents don't know you're here?"

"No," Jerika muttered as she looked down at her lap and fiddled with her blanket.

"So, why come here?" *Maybe she's not that crazy.* She

wasn't acting like a lunatic. Thoughts crept to the surface as he awaited her response. *If she isn't lying about where she's from, what else could be true?*

Jerika took a minute. "Honestly, I don't know anymore. Since I can remember, I've been goal driven. I set my mind to things and I don't stop until I achieve that goal. When I first heard about this planet, I knew I had to come and see it for myself. Then my friend introduced me and my family to Christianity and we converted. As I was growing and learning more, I just knew I had to come here and share my experience with others. When I told others about my plans, they forbade me to come. They never said why; but it didn't matter because I needed to achieve what I set out to do. Of course, I didn't expect *this* to happen," she gestured to the hospital room, "but I'm grateful to be alive."

"Yeah, at first, I didn't think anyone could survive that wreck."

"I wonder if anything did."

"Actually, I did find something as we were leaving," Nevek said as he reached into his coat pocket. "That's why I came today, to return it to you." He only felt the inner lining. "That's strange," he said to himself. He checked his other pocket, but it, too, was empty. He checked his pants pockets as well, but found only his telecom. Naturally, he went back to the initial pocket, but again nothing.

"What was it?" Jerika asked.

As Nevek began to answer her, he remembered his run-in in the lobby. *Oh no! It must have fallen out when I bumped into that guy earlier.* He began to panic as he got up from his chair. "Uh, I'll be right back," he muttered.

Jerika was confused. "Where are you going?"

As Nevek approached the door, it opened. A policeman and a nurse stood in front of him and neither looked happy to see him.

"Yep, that's him officer," the nurse said as she pointed to Nevek.

"He's the one who stole the snacks."

CHAPTER 7

Officer Dwerth loved catching criminals. He delighted in having a crook in his grasp, knowing his prey was powerless because he had all the control. There wasn't a better feeling for him. If he could, he'd lock up the slightest of offenders.

He felt a surge of adrenaline when the nurse pointed out the thief. Sizing him up, Dwerth knew he had the upper hand. He smiled at Nevek through his thick, black moustache, exposing his yellow teeth. His piercing stare never left Nevek's eyes.

"Well, well, well. Where do you think you're going, boy? Why don't we have a little chat?" he snarled as he put his hand on Nevek's shoulder.

"What for?" Nevek said, defensive.

"Well, this nice lady here says you stole some snacks from the hospital, and I don't think she would lie about such a thing. Do you think she would lie to me?"

"I don't know, I've never met her," Nevek said coyly.

Dwerth grabbed his collar. "Don't play dumb with me, you little punk!" he snapped.

"Is there a problem, officer?" Jerika butted in.

Dwerth whipped his head up in Jerika's direction. "Was I talking to you?" He turned his attention back to Nevek. He tightened his grip.

Nevek tried to push him off, but couldn't budge him. "All right, all right. Get off me man!"

"So you admit it then?"

"Okay, okay. I took it," Nevek muttered. "What's the big deal?"

"Stealing is a crime, boy. I'm taking you in."

"Wait!" Jerika interrupted again. "Did you really steal that stuff?"

"Yeah. I was hungry. So what?"

"Well, it's wrong."

"Says who?"

"Uh...the law!" Jerika said as she pointed to the officer in the room. "And more importantly, God."

Dwerth cocked an eyebrow for a second as he looked at her, but quickly looked back at Nevek.

Nevek rolled his eyes as he looked away. He didn't want Jerika to see him. "Here we go again," he said to himself.

"All right, enough chit chat. Let's get a move on." He grabbed Nevek's arm and pulled him toward the door.

"Wait!" Jerika disrupted a third time.

"Oh, for crying out loud. What is it now?" Dwerth sarcastically asked.

"I'll pay for what he stole."

The whole room fell silent. Dwer was taken aback. Without even realizing it, he loosened his grip on Nevek. "Excuse me?" he asked.

"I'll pay the cost if it gets him out of being arrested."

Dwerth couldn't believe what he was hearing. *Who does that?* He looked over at the nurse, still standing in the doorway. She looked as amazed as he was. She shrugged at Dwerth and said, "That would be fine. As long as it gets paid."

Dwerth looked back at Jerika, whose little grin irritated

him. He squinted his eyes at her and nodded as if to say 'okay.'

"Can you get my suit over there please," she said, pointing to the chair on the other side of the room.

Nevek turned and saw the suit. He grabbed it and thought it looked weird. He hadn't seen anything like it before. It was a little dirty still but overall in good condition.

Jerika reached for her suit, then realized her Martian money was probably different from Ceres' money. She felt a sense of embarrassment, but what could she do? She didn't want to ruin the moment. She reached into one of her inside pockets and pulled out a few Martian coins. "Will this be enough?"

Officer Dwerth decided to take charge of the situation. He walked over to Jerika's outreached hand and took the coins from her. He started laughing. "Do you take me for some kind of fool?" he asked as he threw the coins back into Jerika's lap. "I don't accept play money." His laughing ceased and the serious look returned as he glared at Nevek, who wore a surprised expression. "Let's go, kid," he told Nevek as he grabbed his arm once more.

The three of them walked out of the room. Jerika felt humiliated. She couldn't help her friend when he needed it. Maybe he didn't need her help, but she did consider him a friend. At least up until that point. *He'd probably be better off if he never saw me again; especially after this fiasco.*

With his hands cuffed in front of him, Nevek was embarrassed more than anything as he and Officer Dwerth moved to the hospital exit. Dwerth held the underside of his arm. Nevek could *feel* people staring at him as he walked by, without even looking. He could only stare at the ground.

As they approached the doors, Nevek remembered Jerika's device. He had to get it back to her. "Hey, I know this probably isn't the best time, but could you do me a favor?"

Dwerth let out a snicker. "Forget it kid."

"Please? It won't take long. I promise."

"Yeah right. Nice try." They reached Dwerth's squad car and he opened the rear door. "Now sit down and shut up!" he said as he shoved Nevek into the backseat.

Nevek began to panic. His plan wasn't working. "Officer, please," he begged as Dwerth slammed the door. "It's really important. Please? Look, I'm already in the car. It's not like I can go anywhere."

Dwerth sat down in the driver's seat and adjusted the rearview mirror so he was looking directly at Nevek. "Okay, fine. If it'll stop your whining. What do you want?"

"Thank you, sir. I seem to have dropped my slate when I came here. Can you just check the lost and found for it? It's got some important information on it that I need."

"Really? That's it? Ha ha! You're something else, kid." Dwerth opened his door and got out. He couldn't believe he was actually doing this. "And why didn't you get this on our way out?" he asked leaning back into the car.

Nevek shrugged his shoulders. "I didn't notice until we got out."

Dwerth just shook his head. He had a feeling the thief was lying, but played along anyway.

"Thanks again, officer. It's a customized one, so it won't look like anything you've ever seen," Nevek lied through his teeth, knowing he had no other option.

Dwerth walked up to the hospital, and Nevek could hear him talking to himself and laughing. The hospital doors opened and then Dwerth vanished from his sight.

I have to get out of here. This may be my last chance.

He searched the car for something to help get the cuffs off. Nothing. He sat there, thinking about what else he could do. *Maybe I don't need to escape. That'd probably just make things worse.* After brainstorming, he did the only thing he could come up with. He tried for his telecom, but the cuffs prevented him from reaching into his pocket. *It'd just fall out if I was upside-down.* He didn't know where that thought came from, but it seemed like a good idea. He got down on the floor of the backseat and put his feet up in the air. Trying not to kick the ceiling, he put them behind his head a little. He had to hop around a bit, but it finally came loose and fell on the floor. He got to his knees and bent down to pick it up, smacking his forehead on the cage. *Seriously?* He grunted as he finally grabbed his telecom as he texted his sister to come get him.

Officer Dwerth reentered the hospital and didn't even know why. He wasn't even sure what he was looking for. He approached the front desk and asked for the 'lost and found' area. The receptionist kindly directed him to three bins and asked him what he was looking for.

"I'm not really sure exactly," he explained, scratching his head. "I got a kid saying something about a customized slate he dropped. Said it was something unlike anyone's seen."

Slates were the handheld computers on Ceres. The receptionist started rummaging through the first bin. She didn't find anything that matched the unusual description. The second bin yielded the same results: nothing. When she looked at the third one, she saw something that resembled a slate underneath a doll and dug it out. She held up the yellow device. "This looks a little strange. This could be it."

Dwerth snatched it from the woman's hand and inspected it. It really was unlike anything he'd ever seen. "I'm gonna go ahead and assume this it. Thank you for your time, ma'am."

He put the device in his pocket and proceeded toward the front door. Then a thought stopped him in his tracks. *You know, this probably isn't even his. The kid probably stole this too.* The thought angered him more than he already was. He picked up his pace and exited the hospital.

He got to his car and saw Nevek looking back at him. Their eyes locked for a few seconds. Nevek was disappointed to see Dwerth come back empty-handed. The officer got into the car and started it up.

"Did you find it?" Nevek asked nervously.

Dwerth put some dip in his lip and looked around to see if the road was clear. "Nope. Sorry kid."

Nevek was crushed. He just hung his head as they drove away.

Dwerth pulled up to the Zand Police Department, where he was stationed. As a member of the planetary police force, he had jurisdiction over the whole planet. Serving under Chief Haros, he was sent to catch criminals wherever they were.

He opened Nevek's door and let him out of the car. Neither of them spoke. Just silence as they walked into the police station.

The ambiance changed as soon as they entered the building. People were talking, machines were going off; and this was only moderately busy.

Nevek kept quiet. He didn't feel like talking anyway. And causing a scene wouldn't look good. He'd never been arrested before, and he didn't want to give them any reason to make it worse than it already was. Dwerth shoved him into a chair. Nevek let out a sigh as he watched Dwerth take a seat at his rather empty desk.

A sense of relief came over him as he saw Arys enter the building.

Arys scanned the room and saw her brother. She got to him quickly and the look on her face betrayed her annoyance with him. "Have you gone mad!?" she said loudly when she reached Nevek.

Dwerth gave Arys a confused look. "Um... you don't look old enough to be his mother."

She looked over at Dwerth, trying to turn on her charm. "Oh, no. I'm sorry. I'm his older, wiser sister." She quickly turned her attention back to Nevek. "What is wrong with you?"

"I don't know," was all he could utter.

Dwerth couldn't help notice her beauty, but still wasn't biting. "I'm sorry," Dwerth interrupted. "How did you know he was here?"

"He told me."

"I see." Dwerth said as he leaned back in his chair. It didn't sit well with him, but he knew he'd been beat. He just had to smile. He cleared his throat. "Well, since this is your first offence, I'm gonna let you off with a warning, but I'm sure we'll see each other again."

Nevek uttered, "No you won't," under his breath. Arys picked up her brother from the chair and motioned him towards the front door. "I'm sorry for any inconvenience this may have caused you," she said to Dwerth. "I'll make sure it doesn't happen again."

It was a stretch, but Dwerth couldn't help himself. "So, what are you doing later?"

Arys was appalled as she dropped her jaw. "Working," she snapped.

They neared the front when Nevek bumped into a desk. He quickly turned his head to see if Dwerth was paying attention. He was relieved to see that he wasn't. Annoyed, Arys pushed him to keep going, but he couldn't take his eyes off Dwerth's hands. It took a moment, but he finally realized what was in them. *That's Jerika's device!* His eyes widened, and his hands clenched into fists. He was angry, but more shocked that Dwerth lied to him. He cursed under his breath.

Arys snapped him out of it with one last pull out the door. "Let's go!" She looked at Nevek, who was still looking in the station. "What is wrong with you?"

Nevek turned and anxiously grabbed his sister by the arms.

"We gotta go back in there. I think Jerika has been telling us the truth."

CHAPTER 8

"What?" Arys asked.

"Dwerth lied to me!" Nevek was almost yelling.

Arys looked around nervously. "Listen. You gotta calm down." She put her hands on Nevek's shoulder, trying to ease him. "You mean the officer? What do you mean he lied to you?"

Nevek started pacing back and forth, trying to calm down. He tried to wrap his head around what just happened so he could tell Arys about it. "Okay. I *sort of* took something from Jerika and…"

Arys interrupted, "Great! So, you *are* a thief?" She threw up her hands and started walking away. "This is the last time I help you out, kiddo."

Nevek ran up to Arys. "No, stop! Just hear me out."

She turned around and sighed. "What?"

"When Jerika crashed here and I pulled her away from the wreckage, I found something on the ground. I picked it up, but never got a chance to give it back to her until now. But tonight when I went to return it to her, it must've fallen out of my pocket, because I didn't have it. That's when Dwerth came and got me, and so I just asked him to see if anyone found it, but he told me he didn't find anything, but he lied to me because he was looking at it as we were walking out." Nevek was almost out of breath.

Arys was clearly annoyed. "So you're telling me that you couldn't return it to her until now?"

Nevek shrugged his shoulders. "I don't know. I just forgot about it."

"And you're sure Officer Dwerth has it?"

"Arys, I swear on my life."

"How can you be so sure?"

"You can't miss a thing like this. The device doesn't look like anything from this planet. And when I started thinking about it, it's one of the things that lead me to believe she's not lying about where she's from."

Arys was surprised by his logic, and had to admit he was actually making some sense. "Yeah, I did notice a few of the things she said made it seem like she was legit."

"So, I gotta go back in there and get her device!"

"Well, you can't just go into a police station and start demanding it back. You realize how that would look?"

Nevek opened his mouth to say something, but quickly saw that she had a point. "Hmm. So you'll help me get it back?"

Arys sighed. "Yeah, but we need a plan."

Nevek cracked a smile at the thought of him and his sister side-by-side again. It was something he hadn't felt in a long time. "Thanks, sis," he said as they walked away from the station.

Nevek sat at his desk, tapping his fingers on it before class started. It was becoming habitual for him to be unable to concentrate during class. His mind wouldn't stop racing with thoughts and questions. He couldn't focus on any of the material being presented, even though he desperately wanted to get a good grade.

Nevek didn't even notice when Sqett sat down next to

him as the bell sounded. He snapped out of his trance when the professor started talking about the final exam coming up. *Once school is over, that's one less thing I'll have to worry about.*

Sqett whispered over to his colleague, "Hey, Nevek."

Nevek flinched, startled by the whisper. "Oh…hey, Sqett," he whispered back.

"You look a bit under the weather."

"Yeah. Just got a lot on my mind. Haven't slept in a while. I got arrested a couple of sols ago too. And on top of that, finals are coming up."

"You were arrested?"

The professor noticed the two boys talking to each other. "Is there something you would like to share with the class, gentlemen?"

The two perked up in their chairs. "Uh…no sir," Nevek replied, trying to play it cool.

"Then, let's keep the chatter to a minimum," the professor scolded. The two nodded their heads in agreement as he continued to commence the class.

After a few moments, Sqett continued the conversation with Nevek. "Sorry, I'm not one to disobey the statutes of a professor, but would you please expound upon why you were arrested?"

"Yeah, it's a long story. I'll have to tell you later. It was at the hospital where that girl I told you about is."

"Oh, the one from another planet?" Sqett snickered.

Nevek wasn't laughing. He knew Sqett hadn't heard any of Jerika's stories. "Yeah, and to tell you the truth, I think she may be right."

"About what? Being from another planet?"

"Yeah. Certain things have led me to believe that she may not actually be from Ceres. And it sounds weird saying that."

Sqett stared at Nevek with a blank face. He wasn't quite sure what he was hearing. "Are you serious?"

"Gentlemen!" The professor caught them again. "Is there something more important than this class I need to be hearing about?"

The boys perked up again. This time it was Sqett who spoke up. "No sir. It won't happen again."

The professor nodded. He looked over at Nevek. "And you, Nevek?"

He wanted to say 'yes', but it wouldn't come out. The whole class was looking in his direction now. He decided he had nothing to lose. *Maybe he can help me find some answers.* "Professor Kupka, have you ever heard of Mars?"

"No. What is that? Some new app?"

Nevek felt a little embarrassed. A few students even started snickering. He saw the professor had no clue what he was talking about. "Never mind."

Nevek quickly rose from his desk and headed toward the door as the bell rang. He was the first one out. Sqett caught up with him the hallway. "So, what was that all about?"

"What was what about?" Nevek asked as they continued to walk.

"What's this 'Mars' you speak of?"

"That's the planet that girl said she's from."

Sqett paused for a second to think. "Wait. I'm perplexed at the moment."

"Yeah, you're not the only one. That's why I need to find answers."

A confused look spread across Sqett's face. He stopped in his tracks as Nevek continued to walk out of the school.

Nevek only had taken a few steps outside when he noticed Endy walking in his direction. Endy noticed him too, almost simultaneously.

"I didn't know you went to school here too," Nevek inquired.

Endy laughed. "No. I'm just coming to get Zavier."

"Oh, gotcha."

"Yeah, school really isn't for me. Something about hearing someone talk for an hour just doesn't seem appealing."

It was Nevek's turn to laugh now. "It's not *always* like that, you know."

"Yeah, I know. You seemed to have cleaned up nicely since I last saw you. That was a crazy time."

"Yeah, until your best friend tries to have you killed."

Endy looked surprised. "What do you mean?"

"That guy was chasing me because Zavier put our drinks on his tab."

"Wow. What a dillhole."

"Yeah, whatever. I know not to go back there again." Nevek looked up at the building and saw Zavier walking out. "Speak of the devil."

"Oh, you know I love being the topic of conversation," Zavier quipped.

Endy had an angry look as she shoved Zavier. "You're a jerk!"

Zavier stumbled backward, but kept his balance and

threw up his hands. Nevek put his hands up between them to stop Endy from doing anything more.

"Whoa. What did I do?" Zavier asked.

"Nothing. Everything's fine," Nevek replied.

The three looked at each other for a few seconds until the tension receded. "Look. Things have gotten really weird lately," Nevek resumed.

"What do you mean?" Endy asked.

"It's really complicated to even try to explain right now. And you probably wouldn't even believe me if I told you. I was going to try and look into it myself, but now I'm thinking I might need some help. Would you guys be able to help me out?"

"Yeah man. Whatever you need," Zavier said. "You have homework or something you can't figure out?" he chuckled to himself.

"Shut up Zavier!" Endy exclaimed with another push.

"Baby, I'm sorry. I couldn't resist."

"I don't know about him, but I'll help you, Nevek."

Zavier became serious. "Yeah, I'll help."

"Thanks," Nevek said. "I can't imagine things getting any weirder."

Arys ended her shift and was curious to check on Jerika. She passed a few corridors and reached her room. Jerika was up and walking to her clothes. The sudden intrusion startled her.

"Oh, I'm sorry," Arys said. "Were you getting ready to change?"

"Yeah. I'll just bring the curtain around," Jerika said as she pulled it around her.

"I just came to see how you were doing."

"Great," Jerika almost shouted. "I was just cleared to leave."

Arys could sense the joy in her voice. "That is great news. Feeling any better?"

"Yeah. Not a hundred percent, but I can walk around, which is good. Just a little discomfort when I turn a certain way is all."

"So don't turn that way," Arys joked.

"Funny," Jerika declared.

"Well, what are you gonna do now?"

Jerika pulled the curtain away and Arys saw her charred suit. "Uh. Really, I don't know."

Arys looked at Jerika's attire strangely. "You know, we're kind of the same build. Let's go get you some new clothes. You know, at least for while you're here."

"Oh...I don't have any money. Well, I don't have any of *your* money. Nevek saw when I tried to pay for the stuff he stole."

Arys was puzzled. "You tried to pay for him?"

"Yeah. It's the least I could do for helping me out. Kinda like Jesus paid the debt of our sins."

Arys just glossed over the last part. "But you barely know him." Arys stopped herself to explain. "Not that that's a bad thing. I'm just curious."

"Oh, that's what Christians do. Jesus said that it's better to give than to receive."

Arys couldn't quite figure out this generous person standing in front her.

"Yeah, but the officer didn't accept it. Was really rude about it too. I mean, it was real money," Jerika's words interrupted Arys' train of thought.

"Yeah...speaking of him. Nevek thinks he has something of yours."

"Something of mine? What do you mean?"

"Well, he was talking a little fast, but something about finding something of yours when you crashed. He was gonna give it back to you, but he lost it. Then somehow it ended up in that officer's hands. I'm not sure how," Arys explained as she scratched her head.

Jerika had to think about it for minute. "The only thing he could have is my Bible." With that thought, a feeling of relief came over her. She couldn't help but smile. "The word of the Lord endures forever. First Peter one twenty-five."

"Excuse me?" Arys asked

"Oh, sorry. The Bible is the word of God and it says that his word lasts forever. It cannot be destroyed. I was wondering where it had gone. I was crazy to think it was lost in the crash." She looked upward with a "thank you."

"Yeah, but don't worry. We're thinking of a way to get it back for you." Arys said

"Oh, thank you for your kindness," Jerika cheerfully ran over and gave Arys a hug.

"Hey, you're welcome," Arys hugged back. "So I'm assuming you don't have anywhere to go. You can stay with me if you'd like. Just until you go back."

And with that, Jerika's high was stripped away. She let go of Arys and looked down at the ground with sadness. She had to hold back tears. She looked back up at Arys and said, "If I ever get home."

CHAPTER 9

"Okay. What do you want us to do?" Zavier asked.

"I'm still not sure at the moment," Nevek replied.

"So, what are we doing here then?" Endy questioned.

Nevek was starting to get a little frustrated and began pacing. "I don't know. I'm just trying to figure out a way to get that device back from the cop that arrested me."

The eyes of the other two widened. "Wait! What? You got arrested!?" Zavier asked. "Ha ha, crazy! For what?"

Nevek's cheeks flushed red. "Oh yeah, I didn't tell you guys about that. It's a long story."

The other two looked at each other and then back at Nevek. "We're not going anywhere anytime soon," Zavier joked.

"Yeah, what happened? Endy asked

"Man, I thought we were tight. I can't believe I'm just now hearing about this," Zavier added. "I feel like I've done some wild things, but even I've never been arrested before. That's…"

"It wasn't anything bad. I just got caught lifting a snack or two. Just didn't get lucky this time is all," Nevek said.

"Wow. So, what was jail like?" Endy inquired.

Nevek snickered at the question. "I didn't have to go to jail. My sister got me out. I think the cop had the hots for her, so he let me go."

Zavier creased his eyebrows, "You have a sister?"

"Yeah, I told you about her, remember? I hadn't seen her in a while, but she's back in my life now."

"Pssh, man, I don't remember stuff like that," Zavier swatted his hand in Nevek's direction.

"You have a sister? That's cool. I just have a brother," Endy chimed in. "Any other siblings?"

"Nope. Just us two," Nevek answered.

"Glad I'm an only child," Zavier interjected. "Didn't have to share anything with anybody."

Nevek's telecom beeped. He looked at the screen and read his sister's message: "HEY, WHERE ARE YOU? JERIKA'S OUT, AND I'M SURE SHE'D LIKE SOME COMPANY. I HAFTA WORK TODAY." He texted back that he was at his dorm with Zavier and Endy. After waiting a few moments, she responded with 'OK.' He sent her the coordinates and put his telecom back into his pocket.

Nevek looked up at his friends. "Do you guys wanna meet Jerika?"

"Who's Jerika?" asked Endy.

"Oh, is that your girlfriend?" Zavier mocked. "Please tell me you're not still seeing her."

"Oh. I didn't know you had a girlfriend," Endy said. "Yeah. I'd love to meet her."

Nevek gave Zavier a death stare. "No, she's not my girlfriend," Nevek said as he turned to Endy. "She's just a girl I've gotten to know."

Zavier butted in, "Yeah, and she's an alien!" He laughed at his own joke.

Endy started laughing too. "An alien? What do you mean?"

Nevek was getting a little annoyed. "Well, she is an alien because she's not from Ceres. She crash landed here from Mars."

"Dude, you sure you didn't dream her up?" Zavier asked facetiously.

"No, I didn't," he declared. "Laugh all you want. You'll just look like idiots when she walks through that door."

"Sorry but you know that sounds completely made up," Endy said.

"Yes, I know, but it's not. Trust me. Just wait."

The three sat in the dorm room as Nevek tried to keep them focused on Dwerth and Jerika's device. The other two didn't seem to care why they were there, and kept asking more about Jerika, in a mocking manner. Nevek sat back and took the blows, for there wasn't much he could do. He knew he would have the last laugh, though it wasn't really a laughing matter.

The topic changed once more when there was a knock on the door. Nevek jumped quickly from his seat, to get the reveal over with. He opened the door and found a timid-looking Jerika standing there. He invited her in, and she walked into the one-bedroom dormitory.

"Thanks for coming by," Nevek uttered, as it was the only thing he could think of.

"No, thank you for letting me come," Jerika said. "It's very nice of you and your sister to help me out. I hope I'm not intruding on anything."

"No, no. We're not doing anything." Nevek walked toward his friends. "Let me introduce you to Zavier and Endy," he said, pointing to them respectively.

Jerika looked at Zavier, whose mouth was hanging open. As she snickered, he snapped out of his trance.

Endy stood up with a smile. "Hi, it's nice to meet you," she said as she hugged her. Jerika winced as Endy made contact with her. Endy jumped back in dismay. "I'm sorry. Did I hurt you?"

"No, it's fine," Jerika said, composing herself. "Just a little sore still."

Endy didn't know her story, so she was a little confused. "Sore from what?" she asked.

Jerika looked over at Nevek, unsure of how much to reveal.

Nevek shrugged. "She crashed here."

Endy's eyebrowns immediately rose. "What?"

"Maybe I'll just let you tell this story," Nevek said to Jerika as he motioned for her to proceed.

Jerika took a deep breath in and started from the beginning, and decided the abbreviated version would be best at this time. "I left my home planet Mars to come here to Ceres. However, my ship malfunctioned and I crashed. I ended up fracturing a couple of ribs and was in the hospital up until now."

When she finished, she couldn't help but laugh internally at the baffled look on the faces of Zavier and Endy. She looked at Nevek, whose smile revealed he was laughing on the inside too.

Zavier had the first question. "Okay, are you crazy?"

Why do people keep thinking that? "No, I'm not crazy," she replied

"Well I ain't never heard of this Mars before," Zavier exclaimed.

"None of us have, Zave," Nevek said. He finally came near to the other three. "That's one reason I'm asking for your help. Clearly there's another world out there." He pointed to Jerika. "But I'm not sure why we haven't heard of it until now."

Endy seemed ready to believe what she heard, and stood there, soaking in the unbelievable information. Her boyfriend, however, was not so receptive.

"Nevek, man, how do we know she's telling the truth?" he asked his friend.

"Look, I didn't believe it at first, but once I started looking at everything, I don't think she's lying," he explained. "I mean, I saw her ship crash for crying out loud. It didn't look like anything from here."

"Holy snap, I'm so confused right now guys," Endy added.

"I'm not!" Zavier barked as he stood up. "Dude, she's insane. There's no other way around it." He didn't care she was standing five feet away.

Jerika's expression changed from shy to stern—with a tinge of anger. "I wouldn't lie. It's against my religion."

"Religion?" Endy asked

"Are you making stuff up now?" Zavier was just belittling her at this point.

Nevek put his arms in the air to get everyone's attention. "Okay, let's all calm down here," he interjected. He turned to Jerika and placed his hand on her shoulder. "That reminds me, I took your device from your ship."

Jerrika smiled. "I know. Arys told me all about it," she said as she rolled her eyes.

Nevek snickered. He felt embarrassed. "Oh, she did? She told you everything?"

"Yeah. About how you lost it, but you found who took it. That officer I think she said."

"Yes. But don't worry I'm gonna get it back from that

rat. *We're* gonna get it back for you," he said pointing to his friends.

"Really!?" Zavier jeered.

"Yes, we'll help you Nevek," Endy interrupted. "Whatever you need." She looked with kindness and sympathy at Jerika.

"I don't believe this," Zavier muttered as he walked in the opposite direction.

Endy glanced at Zavier. "Don't worry about him," she said to Jerika.

"Thank you all so much. Really I appreciate what you're doing," Jerika said.

Zavier started walking back. "Whatever, man. Let's just get this over with. Nevek, what's the plan?"

Nevek had a blank look on his face as he shrugged his shoulders. "That's just it. I don't have one yet. That's the whole reason you guys are here. Any ideas?"

Suddenly, red and blue lights flooded the room. Nevek got up and looked out the window.

"What is it, Nev?" Zavier asked.

"Looks like someone was just *expressing themselves* on the side of the dorm. I don't get it. Why graffiti a building? Don't people have anything better to do?"

He was just about to turn away when he saw the police car's door open and an officer step out. His back was to Nevek's window, but soon enough he turned around to survey the crime scene. Nevek's eyes widened and his heart started pumping faster.

"What is it, Nevek?" Jerika asked.

"It's him. It's Dwerth. The pig that has your device."

"He has my netbook on him? That has my Bible on it."

She went over to Nevek at the window.

Nevek looked at Jerika, glad to finally know what the device was called. "No, but if we wanna know where it is and get back, now's the time to do it."

CHAPTER 10

Dwerth pulled up to the dormitory with a sour attitude. He couldn't believe his Chief sent him to such a petty crime scene. He mumbled under his breath, "This is ridiculous."

He stared at the graffiti on the side of the building. He spit some excess saliva from his dip as got out. He wiped his tobacco-tinged mustache with his sleeve. As he walked up to the building, he saw what he was sure were words, but couldn't make out what they were. "Looks like garbage to me," he snickered.

After taking a few pictures with his slate, he went back to his car. He got in and dialed the number to the school and got a hold of a painter to see if he could fix the problem.

Dwerth started up his hover car when he noticed some figures moving towards him. Fearing the worst, as any officer would, he killed the engine and stepped back out. It didn't take long before he realized who was approaching him.

"Well, well, well. If it isn't the pipsqueak that got away," he said, being snarky. "I should have known you'd be behind something like this."

"The only pipsqueak here is you, *Officer* Dwerth. If I could call you an officer, that is," Nevek returned the brashness. He and his friends had stopped about thirty feet from Dwerth. Rage was building up inside of him.

"Well, yes, you should since I am an officer of the law.

I'd call you by your name but I can't seem to remember it from our first encounter."

"My name is Nevek. Remember it."

Dwerth didn't say anything in response. Just nodded his head as he smiled at him.

Nevek pointed to the building. "My friends and I didn't do this, and frankly, we don't care who did. We're just here to take something back that's ours."

Dwerth squinted his eyes in curiosity. "Oh yeah? What's that?"

"That device you stole from me. I want it back. Now!"

"And just what device would that be?"

Jerika saw that this wasn't going smoothly, so she spoke up, but in a polite manner. "Look, officer, to my understanding, you have my Bible. My name is Jerika Teverson and I'm from the planet Mars. I lost it when I came here, and was told you have it. So, if you have it, I would just like it back, please."

Dwerth let out a bit of laughter. "This broad's crazy! Funny too. I like her. You should keep her around, Nevek," he said shaking his finger at her.

"I'm not crazy!" Jerika fired back.

Nevek looked at her with curiosity. He hadn't seen her upset before.

Zavier's annoyance had reached its limit. "Look dude, if you have this thing, just give it back and we'll leave you alone. It's that simple."

"Hey, I'm not your dude. Your generation really needs to learn how to talk to your elders. Where's the respect anymore?" Dwerth ranted. He opened his door and began rummaging through his car. After a moment he came out and revealed something to the four friends.

It's the Bible! Nevek realized. "Okay. Just hand it over," he said calmly as he walked towards him.

"Not so fast," Dwerth said as he held up his hand to stop Nevek. "What do I get out of this little deal?" He began taunting them by waving the netbook back and forth.

"There isn't any deal, Dwerth. You took it from me and I just want it back. Please." Nevek was trying to be more polite.

"No, to be fair, I think I should get something too," he said facetiously.

Nevek sighed. "Fine, what do you want?"

"Well, let's see. How about I never get to see your ugly faces again? Does that sound good? Or maybe…"

Zavier tired of Dwerth's ranting. "I can't take much more of this," he said to himself. He looked over at Endy, "There's only one way to do this."

He charged Dwerth with all his strength. Dwerth saw him coming and reached for his gun, but too late. Zavier reached him just as he pulled it out, and tackled him to the ground.

"Zavier! No!" Endy shouted.

As Zavier and Dwerth hit the ground, both the gun and netbook flew out of Dwerth's hands. The gun went one direction and landed near the car. The netbook sailed behind them, hitting the ground and chipping it. The three standing could only watch helplessly as the momentum carried it into a sewer drain.

"No!" Nevek shouted as he ran over to the sewer. He desperately reached in to see if he could grab it, but all he could feel was air. He sighed as he laid facedown for a moment. He picked his head up and saw Jerika in tears. Endy walked over to console her.

Dwerth got up and let out a chuckle. "I guess it wasn't that important after all," he said mockingly. He turned his attention to Zavier who was picking himself off the ground. "And you! That's an assault on an officer, you schmuck. I can arrest you for that." He lifted his chin up in thought. "As a matter of fact, I will," he said as he grabbed Zavier's collar. He took out his cuffs and slapped them on the young man.

Zavier cursed at Dwerth and tried to resist, but the cuffs were already on. The other three looked on helplessly as Zavier was shoved into the back of Dwerth's car.

Nevek wanted to say something, but couldn't find the words. He walked over to the girls and consoled Jerika as she was drying her eyes. "I'm so sorry," he said softly to her. She didn't respond.

They looked on as Dwerth got into his car and started it up. "See you later," he yelled as he drove off down the street.

CHAPTER 11

Nevek laid on his sofa and stared at the ceiling. The scene played in his mind over and over again. Sometimes he imagined himself as the hero who saved the Bible, but he knew that it wasn't real. He felt as though he had let a *friend* down, yet he barely knew her.

A disappointed Jerika had already left. Only he and Endy remained. Endy walked in from the kitchen, a drink in her hand. "I'm really sorry about this," she said for a third time. No matter how many times she or anyone else said it, Nevek didn't feel any better. He must have told Jerika that at least a dozen times before she left; or at least he wanted to. It still couldn't bring her Bible back.

Jerika's grandfather had gotten it for her, she had told them through tears. It had sentimental value attached to it, so the situation was even more depressing. Especially for Nevek.

He sat up and took the drink and thanked Endy. "I can't help but think that there was something we could have done," he said out loud.

"You can't beat yourself up over it," Endy said, trying to be realistic.

"And Zavier! What was he thinking? Such an idiot!"

"Yeah I don't know what he was trying to do. Now I gotta figure out how I'm gonna get him out." She ran her fingers through her hair and screamed in frustration. They both were frustrated and confused. They didn't know what to do.

"I'll see you later," she said as she headed for the door. "Just keep your head up," was what she wanted to say, but she just looked at Nevek, who was deep in thought. She just hung her head as she walked out.

What was going to happen now?

A couple sols passed, but Nevek still felt the effects of the dreadful event. Time seemed to drag on, but he didn't care. He didn't go anywhere or do anything. He even missed a couple classes. All he wanted to do was sleep—a lot of the time he couldn't even do that.

His door chimed. He got out of bed, put on some pants, and made his way to the door. He opened it and saw Sqett standing there. "Hey Sqett, what are you doing here?"

"Hello Nevek. I just stopped by to see if you were doing well. You didn't show up again for class today."

"Yeah, I just wasn't feeling it. I've got a lot on my mind."

"Did you want to discuss these matters?" Sqett said as he walked into the room.

"Uh…not really. Maybe some other time."

"Are you certain?" Sqett persisted.

Nevek looked Sqett in his eyes, "Yeah I'm positive. I'm just really tired is all."

"Yeah, I was going to ask if you were feeling all right."

"Thanks for noticing," Nevek said sarcastically.

Sqett made his way back out into the hallway. "Okay, perhaps then, we can also talk about that netbook you gave me. I've read a few excerpts from it recently. It's quite perplexing."

"Okay. Sounds good," Nevek said through a yawn. He

closed the door behind him and started walking slowly back to his bedroom.

Wait, I didn't give Sqett any netbook. He filed through his memories to see if he could remember. *The only book he would have is...* Suddenly it hit him. His eyes widened and he bolted back towards his door. He opened it and ran out. Sqett showed a sudden fright as Nevek sprinted towards him. "That netbook!" Nevek exclaimed. "That netbook you were talking about, was it from that device I had on my desk?"

"Yes," he said nervously. "The one that I copied the files from."

Nevek was ecstatic. He gave Sqett a big bear hug and even lifted him off the ground. "Thank you!" he shouted. *Jerika's Bible wasn't lost after all!*

"Thanks for what?" asked Sqett.

"We ended up losing that device down the sewer, but it doesn't matter because you have the contents of it! Can you get me a copy please?"

"Um... sure... I guess."

Nevek ran back into his dorm searching frantically for his telecom. He threw couch cushions and pillows around, and hurried from the kitchen to the living room, too excited to think clearly.

Sqett walked back into the dorm and saw Nevek running around like a maniac. He wasn't sure if he should leave or stay. "What are you searching for?"

"My telecom!" Nevek shouted as he ran into his bedroom. He fumbled through his bed and still couldn't find it. He climbed on top of the bed and spied it on his nightstand. He lunged towards it, but missed, falling face first onto the ground. His adrenaline kept him from feeling the pain, so he jumped back up and grabbed the telecom. "I found it!" he shouted as he called Arys.

After a few rings, Arys answered. "Hello?" she whispered, still half asleep.

"Arys! Hey! Is Jerika there?" Nevek said, finally starting to calm down.

There was only silence on the other end for a few moments. "Arys?" he said again.

"Hello?" Arys whispered again.

"Arys! Listen, I'm sorry for waking you up, but I need to know if Jerika is with you."

"Yeah I think so. Why?"

"Tell her that her Bible is not lost!"

"Her what?"

"You know what, just let me talk to her." He started getting the jitters again. His heart was beating fast.

"Hang on," Arys groaned.

He heard some noise on the other end like she was walking. Then silence for several seconds. Nevek hopped up and down in excitement. *What's taking so long?* Finally, Jerika picked up. "Hello?"

"Jerika, it's Nevek. Listen, I totally forgot, but a friend of mine actually was able to copy the files of your Bible onto his slate. And I know it's not the one your grandfather got you, but at least we have the contents so we can get you a copy."

"Oh, that's wonderful news!" she exclaimed.

Nevek heard Arys yell something in the background. Jerika then faintly yelled 'sorry'.

"She's trying to sleep," she said as she giggled. "Thank

you so much. You don't know what this means to me."

"Hey. It's not a big deal. It's the least I could do."

"Oh, it is," she said as she got a little choked up.

Nevek heard her say something in the background. He assumed she was looking upward to her god, which made him happy too.

A beep indicated someone else was trying to call in. He brought the telecom down and saw his mom's name. He brought it back to his ear and told Jerika he would talk to her later because his mom needed to talk. He hung up and answered his mom's call. "Hey mom."

"Hey sweetie. Um...your father's not doing well."

Nevek stood silently for a brief moment. "What do you mean?" he asked.

"Well, he's getting worse. His machines and things aren't working properly, so we're bringing him back to the hospital. Just wanted to let you know."

Nevek was disheartened. When good news comes, bad news is sure to follow. "Okay thanks. Tell him I'll be up to see him."

They said goodbye and Nevek walked out of his room. He had been so lost in his conversations that he forgot Sqett was still there.

Sqett noticed a change in Nevek's countenance since a few minutes before. "Is everything all right?" he asked.

"Yeah... No... It's just my dad. His health is getting worse."

"Oh, I'm sorry to hear that."

"Thank you."

"So, when did you want these files then?"

"What? Oh, as soon as you can. Thank you."

"It's my pleasure."

Sqett took Nevek's telecom and put a copy of the Bible on it. Nevek was surprised how quickly he finished. He took his telecom back and said goodbye.

With all of this finally over, he knew it was time to pay his dad a visit.

CHAPTER 12

Urial Krawse shifted in his seat. The trip from Mars was longer than he expected, but he knew he was closing in on his destination. He was getting more nervous the closer he got to Ceres, but was determined to bring Jerika back home. He worried for her safety, so he said another prayer for God to watch over her.

Urial checked his GPS tracker again. It said he was only an hour out. He was getting tired, but there was no time for sleep. *Maybe Ceres has a nice hotel to stay at.* No. He couldn't let his wandering thoughts get the best of him. He was on a mission and that was to find Jerika. He told her parents he would.

Dwerth fumed, disappointed to see another criminal set free.

Zavier's mom, upset that she had to use most of her savings, paid his bail when she arrived. But she definitely didn't want her son to remain in jail any longer. *He owes me big time,* she thought to herself as she counted out the bills.

Dwerth watched as the bail money was being handed over. He stood up and walked to Zavier, grabbing him by the arm as his mother was looking over the official paperwork she was supposed to sign.

"Hey, what are you doing?" Zavier asked.

"Look, I'm not here for you. I wanna know about your little friend."

"Who? Nevek? Yeah, he doesn't like you," Zavier said with a smart alek grin.

"No, not him, you dipwad!" Dwerth smacked Zavier in the head. "I think she said her name was Jerika?" Dwerth looked around to see if anyone was watching.

"Yeah. What about her?"

"Where did she say she was from again?" Dwerth knew the answer, but wanted to see what Zavier would say.

"She says she's from the planet Mars."

"Oh yeah. Where's that at?"

"How should I know?"

Dwerth grabbed Zavier's shirt and pulled him closer. "Don't toy with me, boy!"

"Hey man, watch it! I said I don't know!" Zavier knocked Dwerth's hands from his grip.

Zavier's mother finished the paperwork and saw the altercation. She pulled Zavier away, and glared at Dwerth.

Dwerth put his hands up and apologized. As they walked out, he yelled to Zavier, "How did she get here?"

Zavier replied, "I don't know. Some space ship, I guess," before heading out the door.

Dwerth headed back to his desk to search for answers. He started typing on his computer, searching for something called 'Mars.' He scanned a few things and to his surprise, found nothing about any places with that name. As far as he knew, Ceres was the only planet, but he'd never really thought about it until now. *Why would that girl say she was from a fictitious place?*

Chief Haros walked into the building and headed to his office. Haros was Dwerth's boss, and a bit older, but the two had become friends over the years. Thinking he might have some answers, Dwerth got up and walked to the Chief's office. The door was open, but he knocked anyway.

"Come in," Haros said as he turned around in his chair. "Hey Dwerth, How's things?" Haros was a bit of a neat freak. Everything had its place and there was rarely anything out of order. There was a small bit of food debris on the slightly overweight chief's floor, but Dwerth was sure it would soon find a home in the trash.

"Eh, not too bad. Just another sol in paradise," Dwerth answered.

"Oh, you'll live. How can I help you?" he said leaning back in his chair.

Dwerth sat down in a chair next to the door. "Well, I'll just come right out and say it. I recently came across this young woman who's quite strange, and it's befuddled me a little."

"*How* strange?" Haros asked with a puzzled look on his face.

"Well, the first time I encountered her, I had detained one of her thief friends, but she offered to pay his ransom with some counterfeit money I'd never seen before. Then, the last encounter I had, she said she was from another world. I mean, that would explain the money she had on her, but when I looked, that place didn't exist. I'm just not sure where she got it from."

"Hmm. I don't know. That does sound strange."

"You're a bit more...experienced...than me..." Dwerth said timidly, hoping he used the right word, "...have you ever heard of 'Mars'?

"Mars?" Haros thought for a second. "No, I can't say

that I have. That's where she said she was from?"

"Yeah. Like I said, it was strange." Dwerth stood up in the doorway. "Sorry to bother you Chief."

"Oh, no bother at all. And I wouldn't worry about it. The girl is probably on some drugs or something."

Dwerth smiled. "Yeah, you're probably right," he said as he walked out.

Haros watched Dwerth leave the office. When the door closed, he picked up his telecom and searched through his contacts. He selected one and put the phone to his ear. After a short pause, he said, "No, no. Nothing like that… But we may have a problem."

Urial entered the light atmosphere of Ceres, which had been created when much of the ice that covered the planet was broken up. He landed his ship safely on the rocky surface. He had finally made it. He got out and stretched his limbs, trying to get his blood flowing again. It was a little colder than he expected, but he had prepared for it. He took in a deep breath to get a sense of the smells of the planet as his dark hair blew in the wind. No foul odors, which was nice.

Urial checked his tracker one last time and saw he was close to Jerika's ship. He was fortunate to have found it when he did. Jerika's tracker, he would find out soon find out, was damaged pretty bad. His anxiety escalated when he saw something off in the distance. He ran to it, fearing the worst. *Her ship.* The ship's condition scared him, causing his heart rate to increase exponentially, but he quickly found a little comfort when he discovered her body was nowhere in sight. He let out a sigh of relief. *Where are you*

Jerika? I pray that you're okay.

Urial looked around the area and didn't see much activity. After a short prayer, he went to search the newfound land. He figured the best place to start was a hospital. *No one could escape that crash without injury. Someone had to have seen the wreckage. I hope someone helped her.* He couldn't imagine her being alone if she was in poor health.

The closest building was a taproom. Urial needed directions, but he couldn't fathom being in such a horrible place. He was clearly going to stand out. He had to find Jerika though. His feet kept moving... all the way into the taproom.

People were busy having fun, hardly anyone even noticed him enter. He felt uneasy as he made his way to the bar. He motioned for the barkeeper, who was serving someone at that moment. The barkeeper finished and approached Urial. "What can I get ya?" he yelled over the music.

"Oh...nothing really. I'm actually a little lost. Which way to the nearest hospital?"

"Wow. You must be plastered," the barkeeper joked, mistaking Urial's fatigue for drunkenness.

"No, just looking for a friend," Urial nervously smiled.

The barkeeper gave him directions, and Urial thanked him. Urial exited and began walking in the direction he was supposed to go. Not knowing the transportation on the planet, nor having any valuable money, he figured walking would be the best way to travel.

His drowsiness continued to grow as he walked block after block. He needed to sleep, but had to keep going. There really wasn't another option.

After what seemed like hours, Urial eventually saw the hospital. He tried to speed up the process, so he jogged up to the front doors. He walked in and nearly collapsed from exhaustion onto the front desk. The middle aged receptionist wasn't amused or or happy with the intrusion. "Excuse me! Can I help you?" she snarled.

"Yes ma'am." Urial gathered his composure. He wiped his face, took in a deep breath, and let it out. "I'm looking for a friend. I think she may have come here. Could you look her up?"

The receptionist squinted her eyes, trying to read him. He was a unique one. "Are you intoxicated?"

"What? No. I'm just looking for my friend. Can you help me? Her name is Jerika Teverson."

She laughed out loud. "Two names? Do you think I'm some kind of fool? You *have* to be drunk or something." Her laughter ceased as she reached down for the phone. "Are you injured in any way? If not, I'm gonna have to ask you to leave or I'll call the cops."

Confusion emerged first, before being replaced with fear. Urial had heard the people of Ceres were mean spirited, most of them very short with people. Judging from the receptionist's reaction, he figured Jerika wouldn't have receved aid here. Not wanting to cause any trouble, he decided just to leave.

Once the doors opened, Urial's fatigue became too much to bear. His eyes were half closed, and he stumbled a bit. He looked to his right and saw a bench not too far away. *I have to get some sleep, even if it's just a short nap.* He almost tripped over his own feet, but managed to get to the bench. He plopped down and instantly nodded off to sleep.

Curious, the receptionist crept outside and watched him as he laid down on the bench. She walked back inside and made good on her promise to call the police.

CHAPTER 13

The hospital room was dreary, without much light. The clicking sound from the oxygen machine was the only sound to break the silence. Arys stepped in and saw her mother standing at one end of the room, looking at her father in the bed on the other side. Arys didn't even want to be there, but her mother asked her to. It had been a while since she'd seen her, and even longer than that since she'd seen her father. She and her mother had met up a few times while she was in school, but since she learned the truth about her parents, she thought it best to stay away from both of them. It helped her to focus as she went through school to become a nurse.

That knowledge made her uncomfortable.

Lyneth let a tiny smile creep across her face as Arys entered. She walked over without saying anything and gave her a hug.

Arys didn't hug her back.

"Thank you for coming, dear," Lyneth said.

Arys simply uttered, "Yeah."

"How have you been?"

"Mom, I didn't come here for small talk." Arys forced herself to be as polite as she could.

"Honey, please let's just be civil for a few minutes."

"I don't have much to say. I only came here to say 'hi' and leave."

"Do you have to work?" Lyneth asked.

"No, I told my supervisor that I'm taking some time off.

Don't want to 'accidentally' get assigned to this room," Arys said with a sarcastic smile to go along with it. "Had some vacation time lying around anyway." She saw her father stir in his bed, starting to awaken from his slumber.

"So, which hospital do you work at?" her mother continued.

"This one."

Lyneth was obviously a little shocked. "Oh. Your father has been here for a while."

"Really? I didn't know that. I probably wouldn't have come to see him, even if I did," she smiled sarcastically.

"Arys, can you not let your father hear you say things like that?" Lyneth scolded.

"Why not? He deserves it too."

"Ladies, ladies! Can't we just let bygones be bygones?" Her father's words were groggy, as he threw his hands up.

Arys turned to her father. "You don't think it's a little late for you guys to start being parents now?"

"Arys," Her father sighed. "I know I wasn't the best father, but I've learned from my mistakes. I wanna do right by you and your brother with the time I have left. For what it's worth, I'm sorry for what I've done. All of it. I just want us to be on good terms again."

"It's easy to say that from your death bed," Arys snarled.

Her father laughed. "I'm not dead yet. You don't know how much time I have left."

"Yes, and Arys, I'm sorry too," Lyneth chimed in. She took her hands. "Let's just put our past behind us and enjoy the time we have."

Her dad tried to direct the conversation away from its

current trajectory. "Yeah, I understand you and Nevek have gotten acquainted again. That's good to hear, although he's not too fond of me right now either," he smiled. "I guess I have you to blame for that."

"Yeah, I just thought he should know the truth. He has the right to know, doesn't he?"

"Yes, he does," Lyneth said. "Speaking of, he'll be here shortly."

"That's good," he said sitting up in his bed. He turned to his daughter, "Can I at least have a hug?"

Arys was still uncomfortable, but gave her father a hug anyway. She wanted to leave, but hearing that Nevek was coming soon, she decided to stay, if only for him.

Nevek got off the CUET and headed toward the hospital. *I gotta stop coming here.* He laughed to himself and shook his head. His thoughts quickly went to his father. *Is this going to be the last time I see him?*

Nevek entered the hospital once more and approached the reception desk. He requested his father's room and quickly received the information. Thanking the receptionist, he followed a few people down the hallway and into an elevator.

Everyone got off at the second floor except for Nevek, who had one more floor to go. After the elevator emptied, a nurse got on. They made eye contact and Nevek nodded to her. He then looked down at his shoes as she went to push her floor. She let out an "oh," as she saw the '3' was already lit up. "Going to the third floor too, huh?"

Nevek glanced back up at her and said "yeah." Her voice sounded familiar. He had heard it before. He looked over at her again. She *looked* familiar too. *Where do I know her from?*

She could feel him glaring, so she looked back over at him as the doors opened. She walked off with her head back down, but then looked up at him again. "Have we met before?" she asked.

Nevek could only laugh. "I was gonna say the same thing. I think so," he said as they stopped in the hallway. It took a few moments, but Nevek pointed toward her as he finally remembered. "I just figured it out. You and your husband brought my friend here a while back. The one that crashed in the field."

"Oh, yeah that's right. How is she doing?"

"She's doing great actually. Just had a few cracked ribs, but she's healed now."

"That's great news. Tell her I said hi."

"I will. I guess I never got to thank you for that night, so thank you," he said with a smile.

"Not a problem. Just lending a helping hand when I can. It was good to see you again. Take care," she said as she started down the corridor.

"You too." Nevek didn't get her name, but was grateful to her. He admired her positive attitude too. *There's not enough of that in the world.* He headed down the opposite corridor to his father.

He got to his father's room and opened the door. To his surprise, his whole family was standing on the other side. *Wow. This is different.*

Lyneth walked over to him and gave him a hug to greet him. Arys sat on the other side of the room, messing with her slate, so he walked over to say hi.

Arys looked up. "Oh, hey kiddo."

"I didn't know *everyone* would be here," Nevek joked.

"Yeah, Mom dragged me into it." Arys rolled her eyes.

Nevek chuckled. He made his way over to his father's bed. "Hi dad."

"Hey Nev," his dad uttered.

"How you feeling?"

"Well, I've been better. A lot better."

All of a sudden, Nevek's telecom started beeping, as he received a text message. He pulled it out and saw Zavier's name.

"Nev, put that thing away!" his mother demanded. Too late. He already opened up the message. "THANKS FOR BAILING ME OUT. SOME FRIEND."

Nevek thought about that for a second. *Why is he blaming me? He was the fool that got himself arrested.*

"Nevek, now is not the time," his mother exclaimed. Nevek realized she was right and put his telecom back in his pocket. He had more important things to deal with at the moment than his idiot friend. "You're right. It was just Zavier. Nothing important."

"Did I hear he got arrested?" Arys questioned.

Nevek's eyes got big as he shot a glare at his sister. His parents were oblivious to the events with Jerika, Zavier, and the police, and he wanted to keep it that way, to not add to the drama. Especially when he didn't even know fully what was going on.

Lyneth looked at Arys. "What do you mean arrested?" She looked back to Nevek. "Honey, you shouldn't be hanging out with these types of kids."

Nevek chuckled. "Relax, mom. Zavier and I go way

back. You wouldn't know cuz you haven't been around. It's also weird you trying to be a parent after years of you not being one."

Lyneth's frustration boiled to the surface. "Listen you two! I know I haven't been a great parent, but I'm still your mother. And believe it or not, I do still care about my children and their well-being."

Arys and Nevek looked at each other, trying to keep a straight face. Deep down however, they knew she was right.

"I'm gonna go get something to eat," their mother said as she stormed out.

"Look, you two should be a little nicer, ya know," their father said sternly.

"Sorry, dad. I wasn't trying to be rude, just stating the facts," Nevek said.

"With everything that's going on, it would be nice to at least be civil with each other."

Arys looked down. Her father made a good point. "You're right. I'm gonna go find mom," she said as she got up and walked out.

Nevek just stood there looking at his father lying in the bed, hooked up to machines, not being able to walk out and leave this place. He wished he had found a cure, but he was sure it was probably too late.

"How are you feeling dad, for real?"

"Well my time is coming to an end."

"Don't say that," Nevek interjected.

"It's true Nev. You talked about *the facts* earlier, this is one of those. I feel my time is almost up."

"I was trying to find a cure for you, but wasn't very

successful," Nevek said hanging his head.

His father smiled as he grabbed Nevek's hand. "I appreciate that, son. But if the doctors who specialize in this stuff couldn't find one, what made you think you could?"

Nevek just shrugged his shoulders. "I really don't know." His thoughts brought him to Jerika. *If it wasn't for her coming, I probably could have found one.* He wasn't blaming her, just the fact of the matter. Then a thought struck him. It was a long shot, but he figured it wouldn't hurt. "Hey dad, have you ever heard of Mars?"

"Mars? No, I don't think so."

"Yeah, that's what I figured."

His father was still thinking about the question. "Well, now that you mention it, that sounds like something Grandpa Ohkly told me about as a child."

"Wait. Really?"

"Yeah, could be. Sounds vaguely familiar."

Nevek was surprised and excited. *Finally, someone who has heard of this planet.* He knew he had to talk to his grandfather and get some answers. It had been a little while since he'd talked with him, but maybe it'll give them a bonding moment.

Nevek saw that he couldn't do much for his father at the moment. He looked like he needed to rest anyway. To be polite, he asked if he could do anything for him. After a head shake, he told his father good-bye and walked out of the room.

As he walked towards the elevator, he pulled his telecom out to text Arys. He told her about their grandfather, and asked if she wanted to go with him. She said she would. He couldn't help but smile as he got on to the elevator. *Maybe now I'll get some answers.*

Urial walked down a dark, unfamiliar alley. His nervousness abated slightly as he saw the sun peeking through in the distance. He had to reach it. After stumbling around a bit, he managed to find his way out into the light. He shielded his eyes to block the intense brightness. Slowly he lowered his arm, and his sight came into focus.

The sunlit scenery was gorgeous. *Too bad no one else gets to enjoy this.* He looked down as red sand blew across his shoes. *Wait, red sand? How did I get back on Mars?*

Urial heard a noise on his right. He looked and saw a house in the middle of nowhere. His curiosity led him to walk to this previously-unknown structure.

Urial took no more than five steps when a distraught woman burst through the door. She fell to the ground, weeping. Before he could say anything, a man came out to console her. They were speaking, but Urial couldn't understand any of it. It sounded as though they were a mile away.

Urial neared the couple to see if he could help. The older couple both looked up at the same time, fear in their eyes. Urial's eyes widened. They were Jerika's parents.

"Where is Jerika?" her father asked.

"I'm sorry, sir, but I haven't found her yet," Urial explained.

"You have to find her!" her mother cried.

"Please Urial. Please find our daughter." It was as if the couple was yelling now.

"Yes, I will. You have my word. I will find her," Urial declared.

"Hey! Are you listening to me?" her father asked.

"Yes. I can hear you."

"Can you hear me? Hey…hey…hey!"

Urial awoke suddenly with a police officer standing over him.

"Hey. Pal, you can't sleep here."

Urial sat up on the bench and rubbed his eyes as the sun was rising. *It was only a dream.* "I'm sorry officer."

"What are you doing out here?" the officer asked.

"I'm sorry," Urial apologized again. "I'm only here looking for my friend."

"Is your friend injured?"

"Yes. Well, I think so. She crashed here. But I don't think she's at this hospital, so I was going to try another one, but I must have fallen asleep."

The officer seemed confused. "You said 'here.' Did you mean Ceres?"

"No, I've come from Mars," Urial regretted saying it as soon as the words left his mouth. "Look, I'm sorry for any trouble I may have caused, but I should be going." He stood up and began to walk away, but the officer put his hand up to his chest to stop him.

"Do you mind coming with me? Answer a few questions?"

"I really should be on my way," Urial said as he pointed behind him and began to walk in that direction.

"Hey! Stop!"

Urial sprinted, the officer closing in not far behind. Urial ran down an empty sidewalk along the side of the hospital. The officer nearly had his hands on him when Urial changed directions and ducked out of the way, making the officer slip up. Quickly regaining his balance, the officer took off again, but with a larger gap between them.

Urial ran into the parking lot, weaving through idle cars to hide. He was successful for a moment, but the officer spotted him again as he darted down another lane. "Stop right there!" he heard.

The officer made it halfway when a car slammed into him as it turned into the lane. The hit wasn't serious, but it was enough to knock him to the ground. He sat up slowly as the driver came to his aid. She apologized and asked if he was okay. He looked in the direction of Urial, but didn't see him anymore.

The officer was angry, but mostly confused. He assured the woman he was fine as he pulled out his telecom from the seat of his pants, dialed a number, and put it to his ear. Almost immediately the other line picked up. "Hey, Dwerth. You're not gonna believe this. Remember that girl who said she was from Mars? I think I just found another one."

CHAPTER 14

Nevek and Arys entered her car. Neither had seen their grandfather in quite some time, but Nevek was determined to find any answers he could about what was going on. He wanted to believe Jerika was telling them the truth, but needed some outside proof.

"I didn't know you had a car," Nevek said to his sister.

"Yeah, I haven't had it that long," she said as she pulled away. "I like it. Sure beats riding the CUET."

"I don't know. I like the CUET sometimes."

Arys just rolled her eyes. "So, do you know where grandpa lives?"

"Yeah. In Elvers," Nevek said sarcastically, wondering why she would even ask such a question.

"Okay. I was just making sure he didn't move or anything." Arys sighed as she began driving.

Nevek's telecom went off. He pulled it out to see who texted him. He didn't recognize the number, but opened the message anyway. It said, "HEY IT'S ENDY. ZAVIER IS STILL UPSET, SO I DON'T WANT TO BE AROUND HIM. I WAS THINKING OF SEEING WHAT JERIKA WAS UP TO."

"Stop the car," Nevek said.

Arys slammed on the brakes, which sent their head whipping back into their seats. They both groaned in pain. Nevek began to rub his head. "Sorry, that's not what I meant."

"Ugh. What did you mean!?"

"Endy just texted me and wanted to see Jerika. Is there any way we can stop by your pod?"

Arys sighed again. "Sure. It's kind of on the way. You could have just said that."

"Sorry. I just wanted to tell you sooner rather than later." Nevek texted Endy the coordinates to Arys' place.

After pulling in at Arys' apartment, the siblings walked in and found Jerika on the sofa trying to understand a television show. "You guys have some weird entertainment here," she claimed.

"Yeah, it's all right," Nevek said.

"Oh, hey Nevek. Everything okay?"

"Not really. Our father's getting worse."

"What do you mean?"

"Well, I'm not sure I told you this yet, but our father is ill. I don't think he has much time left."

"Oh, I'm sorry to hear that. You mind if I say a prayer for him?"

"Uh, sure. What's that again?"

Jerika already had bowed her head, but looked up at his question. "It's where I talk to God. He likes it when we talk to him."

"What kind of things do you say? Does he answer you back?" Arys inquired

"Here, I'll show you. Bow your heads and close your eyes. It's just the traditional way of doing it."

The three bowed their heads in prayer as Jerika began to speak. She prayed that their father would be healed. She prayed for comfort for the family. She prayed that whatever happened would be in accordance with God's will and that they would accept it. She ended with, "in Christ, our Savior's name, amen."

She looked up to see the siblings with their heads still bowed. "That's it," she giggled.

"Hmm, I actually feel a sense of calm," Arys said

"That's what prayer does. Sometimes we just need to talk with someone, and God is always listening. You can talk to him wherever, whenever, however you want. Just let him know what's on your mind. He takes our cares away if we just turn them over to him."

"I don't feel anything," Nevek said. Arys smacked her brother on the shoulder. "Hey! Not cool. You don't even like dad."

"You don't like your father?" Jerika asked.

"Well, he's done some hurtful things to me. Us, really. He's not my favorite person right now," Arys explained.

"Whatever it is, just let it go," Jerika said. "Jesus said to forgive other of their wrongs. If a perfect God can forgive us imperfect people, why can't we do the same? If we don't forgive others, God cannot forgive us. Holding grudges is not a way to a healthy life."

Arys started to say something, but words wouldn't come out. Jerika made a good point, even if "Jesus" and "God" were strange words that made no sense.

After a moment of silence, the door chime rang. Arys went to answer it and let Endy in. She greeted everyone as she walked in.

"So, Arys and I need to go out. You wanna hang with Endy for a while?" Nevek asked Jerika.

"Yeah, that'd be great."

"Yeah, I figured if you're gonna be here a while, I might as well show you around. Maybe get you some clothes that are from this planet," she said as she pointed to Jerika's outfit.

"Yeah. Okay," Jerika chuckled. "I was hoping you could show me my ship too. Just to see it."

Nevek interjected. "Sure. When we get back, I can take you. If I remember where it is. I was a little drunk." He felt a little embarrassed.

"Oh, okay," said Jerika, disappointed.

Endy thought she could cheer her up. "C'mon, let's get going. We're gonna have fun."

Two bodyguards walked Chief Haros down the hallway to Chancellor Cassio's office. Even the planetary leader's acquaintances had to be monitored upon seeing him. Haros had only interacted with Cassio in public settings, but he knew he was modest, so he wasn't nervous in approaching him with such matters. Harois knew Cassio just wanted what was best for the Cerean people.

The bodyguards opened the door and motioned Haros inside. He nodded a 'thank you' and entered. He smiled as he saw the stereotypical scene: a busy politician on the phone. Cassio signaled for him to wait just a moment while he ended the call. Haros passed the time by looking around the office, admiring the scenery.

Cassio finally ended his conversation and stood up to greet Haros. "Sorry about that. Thank you for waiting."

"Oh, not a problem. I know you're a busy man, Chancellor."

Cassio waved him off. "Please, I told you to call me *Cassio*." They both took a seat in the new chairs. "So, what's this problem you were talking about?"

"Well, it's not a problem yet. At least, I hope not," Haros explained. "I know you're younger than I am, but are you familiar with the legend of Mars?"

Cassio thought for a second. "No, I can't say that I am."

"Well, when I was a young boy, a few times my father had told me of a place called Mars. From the way he told it, he made it sound like some folklore, so I never paid much attention to it. I didn't think it was that important either, so I never passed it on to my children, or anyone for that matter."

"Okay, so is this the problem?" Cassio asked, a bit befuddled.

"Well, sort of. As I got older, this legend died off among the Cerean people. I never really noticed anyone even mentioning it until a couple of sols ago. A veteran officer of mine brought up an encounter he had with a girl that said she was from Mars. He's just a little older than you, so I don't think he's heard the story either."

Cassio leaned forward on his desk. "I see. So what does this mean?"

"Well, I'm not too sure, really," Haros said with a puzzled look on his face. "You don't really know if she's telling the truth or if she's just off her wagon."

"Well, let's talk to her. Where is she?" Cassio inquired as he leaned back in his chair.

"Oh, I don't know. I'm not sure if you'd even want to talk with her. See, the one thing about the story I do remember is that the people from Mars aren't real friendly. That's why I don't know if it's a problem yet or not. Just really coming to you for some advice."

"Hmm. Yeah, I say we find this girl and ask her a few

questions. You think you can do that? Just get that officer that saw her. See if we can contain this before it spreads. Shoot, you got me curious now," he said with a laugh.

Haros laughed with him. "Yeah, we'll see. Take care Cassio." Haros got up and said good-bye. He walked out, wondering how he was going to find this young woman.

Nevek and Arys headed off to their grandfather Ohkly's house. As they drove, they reminisced about times when they were younger. They had loved going to his house and enjoying family time. Not so much anymore, as they had their own lives now. The two joked, asking if the other thought he would remember them, and they laughed again. They enjoyed being back in each other's lives.

"I can't believe we went this long without seeing each other," Nevek said. "I still don't understand it."

"Yeah, I don't know. I guess we got caught up in our lives."

"WE?"

Arys snickered. "Okay, okay. I did. I never forgot about you guys. You were always with me. I just hated mom and dad for what they did. I don't know, maybe I thought that you'd be like them."

"I'm *not* like them," Nevek noted.

"Yeah, you're right. I misjudged you." She looked over at her brother. "I'm sorry. Can you forgive me?"

Nevek remembered what Jerika said about forgiveness. If he was trying to be a better person, that was the way to go. He looked back at his sister, "Yes. I forgive you." Nevek felt good inside. Maybe Jerika was right.

"Thanks, kiddo."

"What about mom and dad?" Nevek asked.

"What about them?"

"I think we should forgive them too. You know, just start fresh. While we're all back together again."

Arys started to get choked up. "You're right. I'll tell them when we get back."

"Great." Just then, Nevek's telecom notified him of a text message from Sqett. "HEY. I'VE BEEN READING SOME OF THE NETBOOK. I'M NOT SURE IF IT'S FOR ME. IT'S POSSIBLE I JUST DON'T COMPRE-HEND IT."

Nevek pondered a moment and decided it was cool to see others were actually into Jerika's philosophy like he was. *Maybe we can all learn about this together.*

Nevek texted back, "I KNOW SOMEONE THAT CAN HELP YOU OUT."

CHAPTER 15

The siblings pulled up to Ohkly's home. Nevek was both apprehensive and excited to find out what his grandfather knew. They walked up to the door and sounded the chime, then waited for him to answer. After a few minutes, they started to worry.

"Do you think he's home? This is the last place I remember him living," Nevek said.

"Yeah, we probably should have seen if he's even here before we just decided to make a surprise visit," Arys joked.

Just like that, Nevek's joy turned to sadness. Maybe he wasn't going to find out anything today. *Was this a waste of time?* They waited a few more seconds.

"Should we sound the chime again?" Nevek asked, anxious.

"No. I say we just go. This was a stupid idea." Arys turned and started walking back to her car.

Nevek sighed. "Maybe you're right," he said to himself. He started to follow Arys when he heard a noise. He looked back and saw the door creak open. "Arys wait!"

An elderly woman stood in the doorway and saw the two youngsters, "Can I help you?"

"I...I'm sorry to bother ma'am, but we were just looking for our grandpa, Ohkly." Nevek glanced at his sister as if to say, "We're at the wrong house."

The woman nodded. "Yes, I'll get him." She walked back inside.

Nevek and Arys turned to each other with matching expressions of bewilderment before they ran back to the front door. They weren't sure if they should go inside.

A few moments later, a man greeted them. "Yes?"

"Grandpa?" Nevek asked.

"Are those my grandchildren?"

They knew right away it was their grandfather as they smiled back. "Hey grandpa," Nevek said.

"Well, come on in," Ohkly exclaimed motioning them in. As he said that, he heard some vandals in the distance wrecking an abandoned house. This always infuriated him. "Wretched kids. There's no respect anymore."

Good memories came back to them as they entered. Other than little differences here and there, things looked the same way they remembered. Based on the delicious aroma in the air, Nevek guessed that Ohkly has just finished eating. He tried to ignore the growling in his stomach. He didn't want to get sidetracked.

"So, what brings you two by?" Ohkly asked. "It's been a long time. How is everything?"

"Everything's great grandpa," Arys answered.

"Yeah, we're all good. Except for dad."

Arys nudged Nevek in the side as if to say, "Why would you start with that?"

"My boy's not doing too well, huh?" Ohkly's joy fell. "Yeah, I should probably go see him. I don't get out much anymore." He sat down in an old chair.

Arys pointed to the other room. "Grandpa, who was that that answered the door?"

"Oh, that's just a friend."

"So, how have you been?" Nevek asked.

"Well, I've been good. Body's worn down a bit, but I'm as healthy as can be."

"That's good to hear."

"So, why the surprise visit?"

"Well, dad actually said I should see you."

"He's got good advice," Ohkly smiled. "Ya know, it really is good to see you two again."

"You too, grandpa," Arys said.

Nevek didn't know how to approach the big topic, so he figured he'd just let it out. "Dad said you used to tell him a story when he was little. About a place called Mars. Do you remember that story?"

Ohkly's smile gave way to perplexity. "You came all the way down here for the myth of Mars, huh? Why do you ask?"

"So, there *is* a story?" Arys inquired.

"Yes. My father would tell me them when I was little."

"Wait, there's more than one?" Nevek asked.

"Well, I'm sure everyone had their own versions." Ohkly's eyebrows lowered with suspicion as he looked at them. "How did you hear about it? I haven't heard it in years."

Arys looked at her brother. She motioned for him to be the bearer of the news.

"Well, I met this girl not too long ago who says she is from there. This place called Mars. I had never heard of it before and everyone I asked hadn't either. That is, until I told dad, who said you might know. So, that's why we're here."

"Well, it's true. Some of us older folks had a tale of a place called Mars. I thought it had died out 'cause I hadn't really heard much of it recently, but I guess a few people kept the tale going."

"Yeah, I thought that too at first, but I'm starting to think that it's not a tale."

Ohkly laughed. "Sure it is. Just a fable that had been passed down through generations. That's all."

Nevek explained, "Well, I saw her crash down here, and we started talking, and she said she was a Christian, and I didn't really know..."

"What did you just say?" Ohkly interrupted. His demeanor became grave again.

Nevek looked at his sister in confusion. Arys just shrugged her shoulders. Nevek looked back at his grandfather. "That she's a Christian?"

Ohkly ground his teeth. "She's lying."

"What? What do you mean?" Arys asked.

"Yeah, I don't think she is. She has this..."

"NO!" Ohkly shouted, interrupting Nevek again. "That Messianic is lying!" He slammed his fist down on a tray next to him, spilling the contents onto the floor. You could almost see the steam coming off of his bald head.

Arys and Nevek were stunned. They didn't know of anything to say. They just sat there motionless, looking at Ohkly.

The elderly woman came in from the other room. "Is everything okay, dear?"

"Yes, go back in the other room," Ohkly said loudly, not taking his eyes off of his grandchildren. He pointed towards them, "Now, you listen to me. Do not talk to this Messianic again. Get as far away from her as you can. She'll start telling you lies about her 'Messiah' saving the world. It's all fabrications, you hear? Stay away from her."

"But grandpa, she's really nice and..."

"Get out and don't come back! As long as you are with her, I don't want to see you two again."

"Grandpa, wait a second..."

"I SAID GET OUT!"

The siblings quickly got up and walked out the door. They got into the car without looking back. Arys drove off a quite speedily, just wanting to get out of there.

What's his problem? Nevek thought. *That was really strange.* His mind turned to Jerika. *Is there something she isn't telling us?*

Arys turned to Nevek, "I've never seen grandpa like that before. I wonder what got him so fired up."

"I have no idea."

"That was weird, right?"

"I think it was, yeah. This is all getting too weird. I just want someone to tell the truth." Nevek sighed. "Just means I gotta do more searching."

"Well, I'll leave that up to you then, 'cause I'm tired. I'm going home and hitting my bed. I'll drop you off at your dorm."

That sounded like a good idea. He wasn't that tired, but maybe a little sleep would be good for him.

CHAPTER 16

Urial grew tired of walking, but couldn't stop. *Where could she be? How am I going to find her? How do I know she's even alive?*

No! Urial shuttered at that thought. He couldn't think that. He didn't have a plan or many options.

He found himself at a local galleria, filled with places for people to shop: clothing stores, food stores, and even arts and crafts stores. He was intrigued by the talents of the Cerean people. From tapestry and blankets to glass and metal knick knacks to food he'd never smelled before— some sweet, some with spices he thought he recognized. His stomach growled. *Too bad Martian money isn't any good here...*

He needed to rest, so he sat on a secluded bench. He buried his face in his hands before rubbing his temples. "What am I doing here?" he asked himself. He let out a sigh, folded his hands and prayed.

"Lord, help me in this journey. I cannot do it alone. Guide me to where Jerika is so that I can know she's safe. In all things, Lord, your will be done. In Jesus' name, amen."

Calmness washed over him. He knew God was with him. After a brief rest, it was back to his search. Knowing he'd be here a while, he started browsing the shops again.

As he exited a food market, he caught sight of an attractive female with dark blue hair across the commons. She was with another young woman, who turned around at that moment. His eyes widened. *It is Jerika!* Urial couldn't believe it. He bowed his head and thanked God for bringing them together again.

Urial started to walk over to the ladies when a child ran in front of him, almost running into him. He stopped in his tracks and looked back at the kid as if to say, "What were you thinking?" He turned back to find Jerika wasn't in his sight anymore.

Urial picked up his pace and scanned the area. He searched up and down the walkway, but didn't see them. He turned around and finally spotted the blue-haired girl that Jerika was with, but without Jerika. She was standing, looking at some clothing, so he approached her.

"Excuse me, miss, where is the young lady you were just with?" he asked.

Endy thought it was a weird question to be asked. "That's a weird way of flirting."

Urial was a bit nervous and now starting to worry. "No, the girl you were just with. Where did she go? Where's Jerika?"

What? How did he know Jerika? "I don't know what you're talking about," she lied as she started to walk away. Endy wasn't sure why, but she was getting a bad feeling about this.

Urial grabbed her shoulder. "Look, I'm a friend of hers. I need to see her, please. Can you go and get her?"

Endy pulled her shoulder away from him, and stepped toward the shop. "Okay, I'll get her," she lied.

Urial exhaled. "Oh, thank you."

Endy went back into the shop, looking for Jerika. She quickly scanned the front and saw her exiting. Endy cut her off and grabbed her hand. "We gotta go," she said as they starting walking toward the back.

"What? Why? What's going on?" Jerika inquired.

They stopped and Endy turned to Jerika. "Do you know anyone on this planet?"

Jerika looked confused. "What? No."

"Well, someone knows you. And I don't think he's here to get acquainted."

"Who is it?" Jerika's voice gave a slight tremble. Endy took her by the hand again, and they reached the back only to find the rear exit blocked with merchandise. Endy cursed. "We gotta go out the front without him seeing you."

"I don't understand. Who would want to harm me?"

"I don't know and I don't want to find out." Endy led the way again. "We'll just have to sneak out."

"Should I wear a disguise?"

"Sure. You ever stolen anything before?"

Jerika was appalled. "What? I'm not stealing anything!"

"Well, you don't have any Cerean money, right? You're just gonna have to lift it."

Jerika felt uncomfortable. She'd never stolen anything in her life, but she didn't want to *lose* her life either. She decided to take now, pay later, but didn't feel good about it at all. She wrapped her hair up and put on a hat. *I'm really, really sorry God.* She and Endy headed up to the front. She stopped after a few steps. "Wait a minute! How were we gonna get me something new to wear without buying anything?"

Endy just laughed. "There are other ways. Now let's go."

Urial's back was to them as they neared the exit. They

quickly walked towards the front when Urial turned in their direction. Endy stopped and crouched down behind a rack of undergarments, pulling Jerika down with her.

"Hey!"

"Sorry. He looked this way," Endy explained. She poked her head out to see where the man was. He began walking away from them. Now was their chance. The two ladies bolted for the door and slipped out as a siren sounded.

Urial swung around from looking at some hats to see two people running. One of them had blue hair. *Seriously?* He took off after them, only to run into a crowd of people wanting to see the commotion. After a few steps, he realized he wouldn't be able to catch up to them, so he followed at a distance to see where they went. Then he could confront them.

Officer Talbot was a strapping young lad, the best looking guy on the Zand police force. He took care of his six-foot-one body, ate right, and worked out frequently. The more portly people on the squad made fun of him for being 'something off a magazine cover.'

He walked back to the office with a slight limp from his earlier mishap. Minor injury, though. He planned on walking it off. It wouldn't stop him from performing his duties.

Talbot was still new to the force and wasn't familiar with the Zand station, so he had to ask where Dwerth's desk was. And of course Dwerth wasn't there. *How am I supposed to meet up with you if you aren't here?* He figured he'd wait for him in his chair. No sooner than he sat down, he heard, "You better have a good reason for putting your behind in *my* chair."

Talbot shot up out of the chair immediately. "Just waiting for you, sir." Getting up that quick stung a little, but he didn't want to show it.

"Don't call me 'sir.' It makes me feel old," Dwerth said as he sat down. "So, tell me what you saw."

"Well sir...uh...I mean Dwerth. I encountered a young man outside of the hospital. He was acting a little weird and saying something about finding his friend. He then said he was from Mars, and I remembered that I heard you saying that to your chief. That's why I called you."

Dwerth stroked his mustache as he listened. "Okay, something bizarre is happening here. I'm gonna find out what it is and eradicate it." Dwerth got up from his chair. "So, where's this kid now?"

Talbot was embarrassed. "He got away."

Dwerth looked at him funny. "What do you mean? He's loose out there?"

"Yeah. I went to detain him, but he got away. It won't happen next time."

Dwerth laughed at him. *Some cop this kid is.* "Okay, well let's just keep this between us. No need to bring everyone in on this and get spooked."

"Can I help? I've wanted to be in the planetary squad for a while now."

Dwerth looked surprised. "Oh, you have, huh? Well I don't do partners."

"That's fine. I could just be like your eye in the sky. Except...I'll be on the ground. I could just report to you what I see. It will be good experience."

"Look, kid. No offense. I just don't need you messing

things up. I'm more trained here, so I'll handle it. You didn't even catch the perp right in front of you."

"But please, Dwerth…"

"I said no. Now get lost." Dwerth motioned him out of his sight.

Talbot stormed out. *I'll show him,* he thought as he left.

Dwerth stood, scratching his head. He wasn't sure how to go about the situation. He looked up and saw Chief Haros walking towards his office. Dwerth quickly followed the Chief to his own office. He knocked on the open door. Haros turned and saw him standing there. "Oh, hey Dwerth. Come on in. Just the man I wanna see."

"Hey, Chief. What's going on?" Dwerth said as he closed the door.

"You remember that girl who said she was from Mars?" Haros didn't let Dwerth answer. "Do you know where she is?"

"No, but I'm sure I can find her."

"Good. I got strict orders to bring her in for questioning. You know, standard procedure, okay?"

"Okay. But there's something else."

"Oh yeah? What's that?"

Dwerth stroked his mustache. "I think there may be another one."

"Another one what?"

"Another one from Mars. A…Martian…I guess. This time a young man though."

Haros froze. He wasn't sure what to think. His eyes narrowed. "Are you sure?"

"Yeah, an officer overheard us talking about the girl

and told me he encountered a young man recently, probably around the same age, who said he was from Mars too. Should I be concerned?"

"Uh...no," Haros said. He thought for a moment. *If there's another one, there may be more out there. Who knows how many there could be.* He began to worry.

Dwerth noticed Haros zoned out. "You okay, Chief?"

Haros wasn't really paying attention. "Uh...yeah. Close the door."

Dwerth looked strangely over at the closed door for a second, then back at Haros. "Okay..."

Haros told Dwerth the stories. Stories about the Martians. Tales that eventually got swept under the rug and forgotten. He told him he didn't think they were true; until now. Dwerth, confused, asked a few questions, but Haros was unable to answer them.

Haros gave Dwerth orders to arrest anyone that said they were from Mars, and to not tell anyone else on the force or the local forces. He didn't know how dangerous they were, he said, so just bring them in.

Dwerth walked out of his chief's office with more questions, but also with a strengthened determination to find out more. Haros made no sense, but at least it gave him a good excuse to catch these delinquents. He wasn't sure where to go, but at least he had a lead.

He was going to find their ships.

CHAPTER 17

Nevek was well rested, even though night was falling in Oxator where Arys lived. After much debate, he brought everyone together to listen to Jerika. He'd been interested in her stories for quite a while and was certain others were interested as well. He got out his telecom and messaged his friends how to get to Arys' pod.

Jerika yawned, just waking up as well. Nevek greeted her from the sofa as she entered into the room.

"I still am not used to this time change," Jerika joked.

Nevek laughed a little. "You'll get used to it."

"Yeah, we'll see."

"So, not to put you on the spot or anything, but is there a way you can talk to some people?"

"Sure. About what?"

"Just…you, really. We don't know much about you." Nevek was beating around the bush. "Or what you believe in."

Jerika was surprised. In a good way, of course. "Nevek, are you wanting to know more about your creator?" she teased.

"Hey now. I just get curious about new things. I enjoy learning and I'm not the only one. Some others have taken interest too. I'm not saying we're gonna believe in it, it's strictly for learning purposes." He smiled.

Jerika did her best to hide her excitement. "Yes, I think that would be fine."

They both were hungry so they began searching for something to eat. They were munching on snacks as Arys came into the room, yawning. As her eyes adjusted to the light, she spoke up, "Okay, what are you doing eating my food?"

"Oh, sorry. We just got a little hungry," Jerika said apologetically.

"No, *you* can have some. I was talking to my brother," she said as Nevek's mouth was full.

"What?" he mumbled. "You know I'm good for it. I'll put it to good use."

Arys just rolled her eyes. "Whatever." She went to find something to drink.

Nevek swallowed the food. "So, a few people are coming over shortly," he said, half mumbling.

"Seriously? You can't just invite people over to my house!" she exclaimed.

Wow. Arys is cranky when she wakes up. "It's just my three friends, and it's for a good cause. Jerika is gonna enlighten us with her knowledge and we're gonna discuss some things."

"Well, I'm not providing the food, that's for sure." The other two snickered to themselves.

"So, how was the shopping with Endy? Find anything exciting?" Nevek asked Jerika, hoping to change the subject.

Jerika looked down in embarrassment. "It was okay."

"Oh. Well, we had an eventful time too. I saw my grandfather for the first time in I don't even know how long."

"Yeah, that was strange," Arys added.

"Why?" Jerika asked.

The chime rang at the door. Nevek jumped from his seat to answer it. Sqett stood there, a look somewhwere between nervousness and enthusiasm on his face. Nevek greeted him and welcomed him in.

Sqett had his netbook in hand and was ready for a discussion. Like Nevek, he was curious about Jerika and her beliefs. Jerika finally walked into the room where the boys were.

"Sqett, this is Jerika, the girl I've been telling you about," Nevek stated.

Sqett looked at Jerika with surprise and confusion. "She appears to resemble us," he whispered loudly to Nevek. It was unusual to see amazement in Sqett's face, as opposed to his customary cheerfulness.

"Yeah, I'm just like you," Jerika laughed.

"Oh. My apologies. I just was expecting something... different is all. Pleased to meet you."

"It's okay. I'm starting to get used to it."

"And this is my sister, Arys," Nevek added as she entered.

"How's it going?" Arys asked, not really interested in an answer.

"Very well. Thank you," Sqett said.

"So, what exactly is this Nev?" Arys asked.

"Well, I'm kinda waiting on Zavier and Endy. I know I'm not the only one who has been curious about our foreign friend here." He pointed to Jerika, who just rolled her eyes. "So, I thought we could just listen to her explain herself to us while we're all here."

"Yes, I'm quite intrigued by this book too," Sqett continued.

Nevek laughed as he held up his hand to Sqett. "We'll get there."

Sqett's desire for knowledge, though, overruled his timidity. "I've researched some things since Nevek introduced me to the idea of a god. I've not found anything that asserts one existing. Why do you believe in one?"

Jerika wasn't expecting such a blunt question, but she had heard it asked numerous times. She had answers ready. "Well, first off, we exist. A creation means there was a creator. Nothing just appears out of thin air. It had to be created by someone. Take your netbook for instance. How did it get here?" she asked Sqett.

The question threw him off a little. "Well, the company assembled it."

"Exactly. It had to get built by someone, right? Now think on a bigger scale. This universe, with all the planets and stars and galaxies, is huge. Someone had to have created something so massive. I believe that to be God."

Sqett was confused. He looked at Nevek. "Wait. We're not alone in the universe?"

Nevek smiled. "We'll get there too, but no. Apparently there are other planets out there. How many? We don't know."

Jerika was still stunned by that statement. *How can they not have learned about our solar system?* "Have you heard of the Milky Way galaxy?"

"Yeah, that's the galaxy we live in," Arys claimed. "Astronomy never really interested me, but I know that much." The other two nodded in agreement.

"So, how have you never heard of any other planets?"

No one was able to respond. They just shrugged their shoulders and looked dumbfounded. *That's so weird,* Jerika thought to herself. "Anyway. There is also the concept of design. Everything in this universe is designed for a purpose. From the universe down to the smallest atoms. Look at your netbook again, Sqett. All of those intricate parts all put together just right for that machine to work. If just one part is off or out of place or damaged, the netbook doesn't work, correct?"

"Well...yeah."

"Right. Same with the universe. Everything we see is designed just right. It needs a designer."

Thoughts floated in Nevek's head. *How have I not heard of any of this before?*

"I can give you one more thing too," Jerika continued. "Your conscience bears witness to the creator. When we do something bad and we feel horrible about it; that's our conscience and that points toward the one who put it there."

"Yeah. I usually try to suppress that thing," Nevek laughed.

"What? No. Don't do that." Jerika exclaimed. "It's there for that reason. To make us feel guilty for the wrongs we do." She continued on, "Nevek, have you ever lied?"

"Yeah. I'm sure everyone has," Nevek replied, looking at the others in the room.

"Right. That goes against God's law. Now I know you've stolen before too. That also goes against God's law, among other things."

"Okay. So?"

"When we sin and yield to our desires, we are against God and do not have a relationship with him. Jesus said that whoever commits sin is a slave to it. But there is good news. We don't have to be a slave to sin. We can ask God for his forgiveness and restore that relationship with him. We weren't able to do this on our own, that's why he sent his son Jesus to die for us, like I stated in the hospital. God loves us so much, He sent Jesus to pay the price that we deserved and pave a way that we can be saved from our sins. It's only by trusting in God, asking for his salvation, and being cleansed of our sins that we can be saved. God will then restore his relationship with us and on the Day of Judgment, at the end of time, we will be resurrected with Jesus and live with him in Heaven forever."

This was a lot to take in for Nevek and his friends. He couldn't tell with the other two, but something about what Jerika was saying was making sense. It was still was fuzzy, but he was starting to piece things together.

"So, everyone on your planet believes this?" Sqett wondered.

"No, not everyone. Mostly everyone in my town of Trinion, but not the whole planet."

"Wow. You're a very pleasant person. Are all Christians like you?"

Jerika chuckled. "Well we should be. We treat people with respect and love. Just like Jesus taught. We ought to do to others what we would want done unto us."

Nevek could see she was nice. Maybe too nice. "So, what happens to those who don't believe this like you do?" he asked.

They were interrupted by pounding on Arys' door and the chime sounding rapidly. They looked at each other as Arys' jumped up to answer it. She opened it and Endy ran frantically inside.

"Jerika, you gotta get out of here!" she cried. "That guy from the galleria is here. Zavier is wrestling with him down the hall."

Jerika started to panic. "What? How did he find us?"

"He must have followed us. I don't know."

Arys was still standing by the open door confused. "Wait, what's going on?"

"There was this guy asking for Jerika at the galleria. We thought we lost him, but I guess we didn't."

Endy walked over to Jerika and started to guide her into the other room. Arys started to shut the door as Urial burst through. "Jerika!" he shouted.

"Urial?" Jerika said to herself. She looked over her shoulder to confirm the voice as Zavier ran in and tackled him to the ground in a hail of punches. Jerika gasped. "Stop!" she shouted. Everyone in the room fell silent for a moment.

Endy looked over at Jerika. "Wait. You know this guy?"

Still baffled, she answered. "Yes. He's my friend."

CHAPTER 18

Urial pushed Zavier off of him, knocking him backwards. The stranger got up and looked toward Jerika, happy she was alive. Everyone in the room was now focused on him. The silence in the room lasted a couple of seconds, until Urial spoke. "Jerika. I'm glad you're okay. We have to get home now."

"Wait a minute. Who are you?" Arys asked.

He looked back at Arys. "My name is Urial Krawse. I've come to bring Jerika back home," he announced sternly.

"So, you're from Mars too?" Endy asked, still trying to protect her friend.

"Yes, and I've come to take her back." Urial locked eyes onto Jerika again. "A lot of people are worried about you."

Jerika stepped out from behind Endy. "It's okay, Urial. These people are my friends. You don't have to worry."

Urial let out a deep breath as he began to relax. He couldn't help it. He felt like Jerika's big brother. He always tryied to protect her. Jerika walked over and gave him a hug. Her eyes watered up. She felt relieved to see the face of her best friend. "You came for me?"

"Where do these people keep coming from?" Zavier asked out loud, killing the mood. "And why do you have two names? Your parents couldn't make up their mind?"

Everyone couldn't help but turn and look confused.

"I'm really sorry everyone," Urial announced. "I didn't

mean to alarm you. I was just trying to get my friend back."

"Hey. That's okay," Nevek said as he walked over to Urial. "My name is Nevek." He extended his hand.

Urial shook his hand. "Nice to meet you, Nevek."

"So, are you a Christian too?"

Urial cocked his head. "You know about Christianity?"

"Yes. I've been telling them about Jesus and his love," Jerika added delightfully.

"Yeah, it sounds interesting. A little hard to swallow though," Arys chimed in. "Hi. I'm Arys and this is my pod," holding her hands out as if she were a tour guide.

Urial looked around. "It's a very lovely...pod." He looked back at Jerika. "Can we talk in private?" he whispered.

"Uh, sure." She glanced at her new friends. "We'll be right back."

Urial and Jerika walked into a room. Urial closed the door behind him. "Sorry, I'm confused. What's going on here? We need to get you back to Mars."

"We were studying the word of God. I'm preaching to them!" Jerika couldn't help but be a little excited.

"And they're accepting it? Don't they know about..." he trailed off.

Jerika looked at him, annoyed. "Yes, they are; and no, I don't think so, so if you could not bring that up, I would appreciate it. Whatever you think you know about these people is wrong. They deserve to know about God too. Remember, that's the whole reason I came over here."

Urial sighed. "You're right. This is just a little weird. They're actually listening to you?"

"Yes. I mean, it's still new to them, but they're coming

around."

"Wow. I didn't expect that at all."

"Yeah. I was scared too at first, but they've taken really good care of me since I crashed here."

Urial's eyes widened. "Wait, you crashed here?"

"Yeah. I was in the hospital for a while. Arys was actually my nurse," she snickered as she pointed to the door.

Urial started pacing. "Wow."

"What is it?"

"I overheard Rhine saying that he messed with your ship. That's probably why you crashed." He walked over and hugged her. "I'm glad you're safe." He bowed his head and whispered, "thank you."

"Wait. Rhine!?" Jerika was furious. "Uh! Just wait until I get back!"

Urial began to laugh. "It's okay. Forget about him. You're safe and that's all that matters. That's the whole reason I came. I had to know if you were all right. I guess God was watching out for you."

"Yes, he was."

Urial led a prayer, thanking God for their safety and well-being. Once they were done, Jerika remembered she left her friends out in the other room. "Here, I'll introduce you to everyone."

The two walked back into the room to five sets of eyes staring back at them. "Okay. This is my friend Urial from Mars, as you know. I've known him since I was a kid. We've been good friends ever since."

"So, you're not *together*?" Arys asked what everyone was thinking.

The two looked at each other and laughed. "No, just

good friends," Urial answered.

"So, why are you here?" Zavier asked.

"Well, I knew Jerika was coming over here. Not many people were pleased with her coming, but that didn't stop her. But then I heard that someone tampered with her ship, so I had to see if she was okay."

"Why were people against her coming here?" Nevek questioned.

Urial looked at Jerika. She gave him a warning look. He couldn't think of anything to say.

"They were just worried about a young woman coming over here alone is all," Jerika blurted out. "But I'm truly thankful for all of you and your hospitality."

"Yes, thank you," Urial added.

"So, are you a Christian too?" Arys inquired.

"Oh, sorry. Yes, I am," Urial answered. "I'm from a city called Hevah, near Trinion, as I'm sure you all know of by now," pointing to Jerika. "These are mostly Christian cities, which I am very thankful for."

"Jerika was informing us about why she believes in God," Sqett spoke up. "Why do *you* believe in God?"

"Well...for the same reasons she does. Really it's the only logical view to hold. Even logic tells us that there's a God. Things such as logic and mathematics are truths in this universe. They're ever constant. These truths can only come from the one that is absolute truth who designed this vast universe we live in."

The Cereans wanted to learn more, but didn't really know what to ask. They were still processing what they'd heard already.

Arys looked at the time. "Hey, Nev. We should probably go see Dad."

"You're right," Nevek said as he got up from his seat. "Uh, Urial right? It was nice to meet you, but we gotta go visit my dad in the hospital.

"Oh, okay. Is everything all right?"

"No. He's ill. We don't know what it is or how much time he has left."

"I'm so sorry to hear that. I will pray for you and your family."

Nevek nodded as he waited for Arys to change clothes. After a few moments, she came back out. "So I guess you guys can stay here. Just be kind to my place." Then she and Nevek bolted out the door.

Jerika smiled and called out "I'll take care of it." She figured she would get Urial caught up with everything that was going on. She was sure the others had more questions too.

Dwerth was getting tired. He had been out looking for the Martians without any luck. He went to Nevek's dorm, the hospital the Martian girl stayed at, and everywhere in between. He didn't think she went to another part of the planet, but that was his next step. He needed to pan out his search.

He walked into the police station to regroup and get something to eat. After quenching his hunger, he plopped down at his desk, trying to think of everything he knew about Jerika and her friends. *What are they hiding? Where could they have gone?* Frustration mounted when nothing came to mind.

He was looking through some files on his netbook

when he heard Haros call for him to come to his office. It took all he had to get out of his chair and walk there, as he was beginning to get tired. He walked in and closed the door behind him. Haros finished up some work and then looked out into the station as if to see if anyone was watching them. "You find those Martians yet?" he uttered.

"No, sir," Dwerth answered as he sat down in front of the desk.

"Woah. You don't look so good."

"Yeah, I don't think I've slept in a few sols. Been trying to find that girl." Dwerth leaned back in his chair and rested his head on top of it.

"Look. I know we'll find them. You're good at what you do, Dwerth."

"How do we even know they're still here?"

Haros thought for moment. "Nah, don't think like that."

Dwerth was still looking up at the ceiling. "Well, I haven't heard anything about them in a while."

"Hmm. Yeah, maybe they left already. Just seems too good to be true. I guess it is possible. Tell you what. Take some time off and go get some rest. I'll take a crack at it for a while."

"Thanks. I'll do that, Chief."

Dwerth got up from his chair as a knock came on the door. Talbot entered with a smile on his face. "Dwerth, I think we got a lead."

Haros spoke up from his desk. "Dwerth is taking a leave now. Tell me about this lead."

"Oh, sorry Chief. This is about a secret case Dwerth and I are on."

"You mean the Martian mission, kid?" Dwerth asked.

"Chief already knows about it. He's the one that put me on it. And I told you, you're not on this case."

Haros laughed. "Gentlemen. We're all family here. Let the boy work with you Dwerth. He may learn a thing or two, you know. Now officer, what lead are you talking about?"

"Well, I just got a call from a lady that said her son and his friends stumbled upon... what they called 'some unidentified space ships' in a remote field. I think it's worth looking into. I think it could be our Martians or whatever you call them," Talbot explained.

"Well, Dwerth. I guess they haven't left after all." Haros said with a smile on his face. He looked over at Talbot, "Let's go, son. Lead the way."

CHAPTER 19

Nevek and Arys made their way into their father's hospital room. As they came through the door, they heard the sobbing of their mother, whose hand held tightly to their father's. "What's wrong?" Nevek asked.

"He doesn't have much time left," Lyneth answered, as she began to regain her composure for her children's sake.

They looked with shock and sadness at their father, his face drained of color, his body significantly thinner. He opened his eyes and a smile broke on his unshaven face as he saw them. "We're here, Dad," Nevek said.

"I know...and it's...wonderful," he strained, his words coming out as more of a loud whisper. Breathing took up most of his energy.

"It's okay, Dad. You don't have to talk," Nevek assured him.

They were surprised at how rapidly his health was declining.

"We're here for you," Arys said, taking a hold of his hand as well. She started to get choked up. "I know I haven't been too fond of you for a long time." She looked over at her mother. "Either of you. But I just wanted to say I'm sorry. I'm sorry for the way I acted. I forgive you guys and I hope you can forgive me too."

"Me too," Nevek added. "Let's just put this behind us and start over." He looked at Lyneth. "I'm sorry, Mom. I forgive you." He reached over and hugged her. Her tears returned as she thanked him. Arys put her father's hand to her cheek as he thanked her as well. Her eyes started to water as well.

"I'll leave you guys alone for a little bit. I'll be right back," Lyneth said as she got up from the chair and walked out.

The siblings stood next to the bed, struggling to know what to say as they looked at their dying father. The sight made them feel completely helpless inside. The beeping from an apparatus connected to their father by wires and tubes served as the background to their silence.

"I'm gonna miss you dad." Nevek choked up, but didn't want to show it, so he looked towards the ceiling and walked away for a moment.

"I'll miss…you too, Nev." He slowly turned to his daughter. "You…too, Arys. Thank you for…being here."

"Of course, Daddy."

Nevek came back to the bed and looked his dad in the eyes. "Have you ever heard of Christianity?"

"What?" Arys let out a strange look in her brother's direction.

"No, son… Why?"

Nevek thought for a second. *Maybe this is the cure I was trying to find.* "Dad, there is a god out there. He loves us and he sent his son to die for us. We can restore the broken relationship we have with him."

"What are you doing?" Arys whispered.

"Do you believe in the god, Dad?" Nevek took his father's hand. He could tell he was confused, though he couldn't be sure how much of the confusion came from his worsening condition.

His father looked back at him. "No... that's okay."

He didn't know why, but he was stunned by his father's response.

Arys took her brother's arm and walked to the other side of the room. "What was that?"

"I...I don't know. I panicked. I couldn't think of anything to say."

"So, you started to talk to him about the god?"

Nevek just shrugged his shoulders.

"Sorry, but I don't think that was a good idea. He doesn't know everything we do," Arys said. Nevek agreed. The beeping on the machine next to their father started increasing rapidly. Nevek ran over to his father's bedside. "Dad?" No response. Arys walked over with her hand over her mouth. Nevek's heart started racing as he looked at his father. "Dad?" He turned to Arys. "What's going on?"

"Nev...he's gone," she said faintly.

"What!? No! Dad can you hear me?" He began pounding his fists on the bed in frustration. "Come on, Dad!"

Arys walked over to him and wrapped her arms around her brother. A nurse walked in to assess the situation. Nevek couldn't stay in there, couldn't breathe. He pushed his sister off of him and sprinted out. He ran to the elevator and snuck in as the door was closing. He leaned up against the back wall, looking upward. He was devastated, but anger welled up inside of him, keeping his tears at bay. He struggled to make sense of things, struggled to keep control of his emotions. *No. This can't be happening. Why, Dad?*

But he couldn't figure out if he was more upset with his dad's leaving, or his rejecting any discussion about the god.

Nevek's adrenaline kept him running towards the

CUET. He reached it as the doors were opening. He walked into the empty car, found a seat, sat down on the edge of it, and slid to the ground. He buried his head between his legs, his hands on the back of his head, and he sobbed. He had never experienced anything like this before. He let everything out the whole ride.

As the tram approached his stop, Nevek tried to calm his nerves. He decided to go back to Arys' place to see some familiar faces—but he also wanted to be alone. He didn't really know what he wanted. Too many thoughts running through his head. At this point, he was just going through the motions.

After what seemed like forever, he arrived at his sister's pod. He made his way up to her door just as his friends were leaving. He tried to hide from them, but it didn't work. Endy caught sight of him out of the corner of her eye. "Hey Nevek. Everything okay?" Endy asked nervously.

"He's gone," was all he could say.

"Oh, I'm so sorry," she said as she gave him a hug. Zavier and Sqett also said their condolences.

"Thanks. I kinda just wanna be left alone now."

"That's fine, brother. We get it," Zavier said.

"Well, come on inside," Jerika said. "There's no reason to be out here."

The others said their good-byes and Jerika led Nevek into Arys' pod. He was like a robot as he sat down on the sofa, showing no emotion. He just stared down in front of him. Jerika didn't know what to do but look at him.

Urial came in from the other room. "Hey, Nevek. Back so soon?" Jerika gave him a dirty look. Urial just shrugged his shoulders.

"What happens when we die?" Nevek asked out of the blue, still looking ahead.

Urial's face registered shock and embarrassment as he finally recognized what was going on. He'd never been asked this question before. "Well…um…those faithful to God will be rewarded with a paradise and after Judgment Day, go to live with him. Much like a 'rest' from their labors."

"Nevek, I am really sorry about your dad," Jerika added.

Nevek finally broke his trance and looked over at Urial. "What about those that aren't faithful to God?"

"Well…the faithful ones are cleansed of their wickedness and the unfaithful are punished for their wickedness."

"Punished? Punished how?"

Urial knew he had to give Nevek the truth. "Well, the Bible says those that serve God will be with him forever. Those that don't serve him, He punishes forever. A never-ending torment of fire for rejecting him and his offer of salvation."

This wasn't something Nevek wanted to hear. He became very upset. "So, he just endlessly tortures them?"

"Yes. The Bible calls this place 'Hell.'"

Jerika wrung her hands with nervousness.

Nevek felt his rage building inside of him. "So he burns people forever? I thought he loves us?"

Jerika tried to get back into the conversation. "Yes, He does but you see…"

Nevek cut her off. "That doesn't sound very loving, does it?"

Urial spoke again and put his hands up. "Nevek, calm down. We're just…"

"Calm down? You're saying that this god killed my dad and now because he didn't serve him, he's gonna punish him forever? How dare you!" he said as he stood up. "Get out of here! I don't ever want to see you guys again!"

Jerika tried one last time. "Nevek listen…"

"I SAID GET OUT! Leave my planet! Go back to wherever you came from!"

Urial got up, took Jerika by the hand and led her out. He didn't look back, but Jerika couldn't look forward. She felt awful. *He didn't really mean it. He couldn't.*

The sun was going down on a quiet, brisk evening. Not much was going on in this modest neighborhood in Valtux, except for the arrival of two police cars, whose lights seemed to illuminate the whole block. Chief Haros and Talbot arrived at the home of a woman who had called the station. They both got out of their cars and walked up to the front door. The woman met them at the door before hey could knock.

Haros took the lead and got the story from the woman. Her son and some friends had found two spacecrafts in a barren part of the city. Haros stayed with the woman as Talbot went to speak with the son.

Talbot asked the kid some basic questions; what did he see? and where did he see saw it? As he was taking notes, he decided it would be better if the kid could just show him where he saw these spacecrafts. After securing the mother's permission, the three got in the car and went on their way.

They arrived at a parking area and walked over to an

open plain where they saw the wreckage. They were astonished when they saw the remains of a battered ship. It still smelled like charred metal. The two officers went to investigate, the young lad not far behind.

"I've never seen anything like it," Talbot said aloud.

They walked around the crash site, trying to understand it all. Haros walked around the rear while Talbot inspected the left side. He crouched down and ran his hand along the gashes of the ship. "How did anyone survive this?"

"What I wanna know is how has nobody seen this before?"

Talbot noticed the boy wasn't in sight. He started to search around for him when he heard the words: "The other one is over here."

The officers walked to the other ship which was fully intact. The sun was just about to set, but the light displayed much greater detail on the uncharred vessel. More designs and machinery to look at. Talbot admired the craftsmanship as he felt the cold metal, welded to the inside control panel. He really wanted to take it for a ride.

Haros was busy looking for a way in. He went around the back as before, but wasn't successful. *It must be locked.*

"It's like they have a different technology than we do, Chief," Talbot said.

"Yeah, maybe," Haros replied.

"Whose are those?" the boy asked.

Haros nearly forgot the child was still there. He didn't want this getting out to the public. "It's just for entertainment, son. No need to worry. Don't tell anyone about this, okay?"

The boy thought for a minute and agreed. Haros told

him to go wait by his car and he'd take him home shortly. As the boy ran over, he almost fell, tripping on something.

"Listen, Talbot, you mind staying out here awhile? The ships are still here, so that means the Martians are too. They'll come back eventually."

"Yeah. Sure, Chief. Not a problem."

"Good. And if you see 'em, lock 'em up for a while."

Urial and Jerika followed Urial's tracker back to his ship. Jerika couldn't take her mind of Nevek, and her heart ached for what he was going through. But she couldn't do anything about that now. It was time to go home.

"I can't get over how sols go by so quick here," Urial said.

"That's what you're thinking about?" Jerika asked in a stern tone. "Our friend is hurting right now."

"*Our* friend? I barely know him," Urial snickered. Jerika angrily stared back him. "Okay, sorry, you're right, but there's nothing we can do. You saw how he reacted."

"There's got to be something!"

Urial stopped and grabbed Jerika's arm. He placed his hands on her shoulders. "Look, we did all we could. We preached to people that have never heard of God before. We planted the seed, it's up to God to work in their lives now." Jerika dropped her head. "Hey, I'm proud of you for what you did. That took a lot of courage. It's just up to God now. We're clearly not wanted here anymore."

"You're right," she said quietly with a hint of sadness

The two started walking again. They said a prayer for Nevek, his family, his friends, and his planet. They prayed that these people would know who God is and that he would work in their hearts. As they ended the prayer, Urial stopped. He pointed to his ship. "Look, there's the way out."

He got Jerika to smile. "Let's go home," she said. They took one step and felt a hand on their shoulders. Urial was spun around. His eyes gaped open when he saw the officer from the hospital.

"Not so fast, Urial. We never got the chance to get to know each other."

CHAPTER 20

Nevek sat alone in his favorite taproom. He didn't return to the one in Elvers, for fear of running into that muscular drunk again. No sooner had he sat down at a table in the back, than one of the two bulbs went out over him, perfectly reflecting his mood. He tuned the world out. He hadn't talked with anyone in a couple of sols and hadn't slept since then either. He was beyond the point of inebriation and still drinking. And he didn't care.

Arys tried to contact him, but Nevek didn't respond. He wasn't going to respond to anyone. He just wanted to be left alone.

He kept replaying his father's death over in his head. He couldn't get it out; not that he wanted to. He played out scenarios in his head about how he could have been a better son. How his dad could have been a better father. What else they could have achieved together. As he finished his drink, Jerika entered his mind. And with her, Urial, and what he said. He slammed his glass down at the thought, cracking it. "He was a good person!" he said out loud. A few people around him turned and looked curiously.

Zavier walked in the taproom at the opportune moment to witness Nevek's outburst. He ordered a drink from the barkeeper, and made his way over to his friend. He took a seat at the dimly-lit table across from Nevek. "I had a feeling you'd be here."

"Go away, Zave. I just wanna be alone," Nevek murmured, still staring into his empty, broken glass.

"I just ordered a drink, so I can't leave yet," he said with a snicker.

Nevek sighed. "Fine, just don't talk to me."

Zavier snickered again, but verbally agreed as his drink arrived. The two sat there for a few minutes in silence, Zavier sipping on his drink and Nevek laying his head on the table with his arm for a pillow. Zavier finally broke the silence, "Okay, this is awkward."

"No one asked you to come here." Nevek's voice was muffled in his arm.

"Actually, your family asked where you were and asked me to find you. I knew you'd be here. That's the only reason I came. You know the funeral is in a few hours at dawn."

"I'm not going."

Zavier laughed. "You're not going to your own father's funeral? Sorry man, but you must be joking."

Nevek didn't say anything.

Zavier tried a more serious approach. "C'mon man. Everybody is gonna be there. We're here for you, Nev."

Nevek snickered. "Not everyone, fortunately."

"What do you mean? Who's not gonna be there?"

"The ones from Mars," Nevek mocked.

"I don't understand, man."

Nevek sat up. "They have weird beliefs, so I told them to go home."

"Hold up! Seriously?" He saw Nevek look down and nod. "Ha ha! That's what I like to hear!" He slammed his hands down on the table. "Woo! I can drink another to that." He yelled an order to the barkeeper.

"No thanks, Zave. I don't think I can drink anymore."

Nevek put his head back down on the table.

"Oh. No, this is for me. Those two were kind of getting annoying. Good riddance to 'em." He took a sip. "Honestly, I didn't know how much longer they would stay anyway. Whatever though. Now things can go back to the way they were and we can forget they even existed. We can be late to the funeral, right?"

The time for the funeral arrived.

Zavier was half-carrying Nevek, who could barely stand, let alone walk, as they neared the funeral parlor. Almost immediately, they were greeted by Arys and Endy. "Thank you for finding him," Arys said to Zavier. "Where were you!?" she almost shouted at her little brother.

Nevek looked at her, fighting a battle to keep his balance with the intense headache and untold amount of alcohol in his system. After a brief pause, he started to talk, but vomit spewed from his mouth onto the ground. His friends jumped back, not wanting to catch any shrapnel.

"Are you serious? You were drinking! What is wrong with you?" she scolded.

"Hey, calm down. People grieve differently," Zavier explained holding his free hand out to Arys. "He'll be fine. Has it started yet?"

"No," answered Endy.

"So, then we're good. Nothing to worry about," he said as he walked past the ladies. Nevek staggered behind without saying a word.

They all walked into a small, well-lit room as the director stood up to start the memorial. He approached the podium and welcomed the few people there for attending.

Nevek's father was an only child, and only had a few friends, so the director was able to talk without any amplification.

After the initial greetings, he stated why they were there and said a few words about the life of the deceased that he'd received from Lyneth and a few others. He then turned the floor over to anyone who had a story about him; whatever it may be.

Most of the stories were about how they met or a something funny that happened. Most of the people that spoke were his friends and a few distant relatives. Nevek also watched as his mother went up and told of his father's character. She then started to weep and had to walk off.

Nevek then heard someone he didn't know tell a couple of stories. He assumed she was one of his father's friends. He even smiled once. The woman then grabbed his attention as she started to talk about the life beyond this one. She rhetorically asked what was on the other side. This, of course, brought back Nevek to what Urial and Jerika had told him. Rage started to build up inside of him anew. He began nervously shaking his leg. It grew faster and more violent the more he thought about it. He couldn't handle it anymore and got up to walk into another room.

Arys got up to go after him, but felt a hand on her shoulder. "Let me go talk to him. He might not talk to you," Endy whispered. Arys agreed and sat back down as Endy climbed over her.

Nevek entered a side hallway while Endy came behind him. He didn't even have time to think before she asked him if he was okay. "Why won't people just leave me alone?" he asked out loud.

"You know we can't do that. We're your friends."

"If you were my friends, you'd respect my wishes," he snarled.

Endy bit her bottom lip and looked down in disappointment. "You know, I didn't really have many friends until I met all of you. Now I see this little group we've made and we're all close. I'm enjoying the new company and getting to know you." She walked up to him and gave him a hug. She spoke softly into his ear, "We know what you're going through. Just know we're here for you."

Nevek only raised one arm in the embrace.

Endy let go and their eyes met. Nevek was felt awkward. For some reason, Endy was becoming appealing to look at. He hadn't seen her like this before.

Then she kissed him.

What is she doing? Nevek knew it was inappropriate, but he couldn't push away. It was like he was paralyzed for a second, until he finally backed away.

"I'm so sorry," she said almost immediately.

"Yeah, me too."

"I don't know what came over me," she said, embarrassed.

"Look, Zave is my best friend. He *cannot* find out about this." Nevek was definitely confused.

"Right. I'm just gonna…go back out there," she pointed behind her.

Endy walked toward the door and as it opened, Nevek said, "This never happened."

If Nevek wasn't sober before, he was now. Endy sat back down as Nevek entered back into the main room. He glanced at Endy as he took his seat, but she was looking straight ahead. The director got back up and asked if anyone else wanted to speak, but no one responded. He then said some closing remarks and informed them about the room behind them where food would be served and invited them to stay and socialize before ending the service.

Folks gathered into the large room with the complementary food and beverages. It wasn't much but, no one complained. They were only there to mingle for a while and enjoy the company of one another.

Nevek was hungry, but that kiss had his focus. He couldn't get it out of his mind as he sat down. He didn't even like Endy that way. Or did he? He really hadn't thought about it until now. Arys broke his concentration when she sat down next to him. "Are you okay?"

"Yes...no...I don't know."

"Everything will be all right. We'll get through this. Hang in there," she said with her hand on his shoulder.

Ohkly made his way over to his grandchildren. Arys saw him coming from a distance. "Grandpa's coming. That's my cue to leave," she said, as she left her brother alone.

Nevek watched as Ohkly sat down. At his old age, it was a bit of a struggle. "Hey Nevek."

"Hi, grandpa."

"I'm sorry about your loss. Your dad was a good man. He didn't deserve to go out like that."

"Thanks."

"So, did you cut ties with those Messianics?" Ohkly tried to change the subject.

"Yes, sir."

"You did?" Ohkly was a bit surprised. "That's good to

hear, son."

"They have weird beliefs," Nevek blurted out.

"Ha ha. I knew you'd see it. Nothing good comes from them. Just like Salem."

"Who's Salem?"

Zavier sat down next to Nevek at that moment.

"Oh...just an old buddy of mine. Forget I mentioned him. Old news. Don't need him. Just like those Messianics. Free your mind of them."

Ohkly got up from his seat. "Take care, Nevek." He saluted him and left.

Who is Salem?

"Hey man, just checking in on ya." Zavier patted Nevek on the back. "Who was that?"

"That was my Grandpa Ohkly."

"Did I hear him talking about the Martians?"

"Yeah. He said to stay away from them."

"Really? Smart man. Words of wisdom," Zavier said with a chuckle. "I told you they were no good."

"Yeah. I think he said he knew one."

"Hmm. That's weird." Zavier stroked his chin.

"I gotta find him."

Zavier looked over at his friend like he was looking at a ghost. "Excuse me?"

"I gotta find this 'Salem.' He may have answers."

"Wait. Hold up. Answers for what? Just leave it alone. Urial and Jerika are already on their way home. They're gone. No need to pursue this any further. Let's just get back to how things were."

"Sorry, dude. I'm already interested now. I have to talk to this guy. You coming with me?"

"What!? No. No, I'm not going with you because you're not going either. Give it a rest, man. This guy is gonna be old, right? How do you even know if he's still alive?"

Nevek shrugged his shoulders. "I don't, but I have to find out," he said as he got up and walked out.

CHAPTER 21

"How long are you going to keep us in here!?" Jerika shouted from her holding cell, visibly upset.

"It's no use yelling," Urial said, sitting on the ground beside her.

"They can't do this to us! We didn't do anything wrong!"

Haros was sitting in his office listening in on his slate. He chuckled to himself. Dwerth entered the room carrying a cup of coffee. "So, I heard you got them."

"Yeah they've been in that cell for a few sols now."

"A few sols? Why so long?"

"Waiting for Chancellor Cassio. He wanted to have a talk with them."

"Oh." Dwerth went silent for a moment. "So, when is he going to talk with them?"

"Don't know. Haven't told him we've got 'em yet."

Dwerth laughed. "So, how long are you going keep them in there?"

"I guess I could call him now. Maybe they've suffered enough." Haros took out his telecom and dialed the number to the Chancellor of the planet. After a brief conversation, he hung up and tossed it onto his desk. "He said he'd be here shortly." He looked up at Dwerth, "So, how was your time off?"

"Great," he said sipping some coffee. "Much needed, thank you." He raised his cup to Haros.

"Good to hear."

Dwerth decided to take a seat. "So, did I miss anything while I was gone?"

"Yes, actually. Since it was Talbot that caught our intruders, I promoted him to our squad."

"Really?"

"Yeah. He was quite delighted. He still has some work to do to prove himself, so we'll see how he does on the next level. I think he'll do fine though."

Dwerth just smiled in his seat. "So, when should I talk to these Martians?"

"Oh, you're not on this case. I took Talbot off, too. We'll just wait and see what the Chancellor wants to do with them."

"Well, okay then. I'll get back to work."

Nevek took the CUET to the nearest cafetorium. Before he left the funeral, he asked his mother about Salem, but she didn't remember much. Only that he was a teacher. He sat down at a computer and searched for Salem. Not much came up, so he refined his search to educators.

His telecom buzzed a few times. It was Arys seeing if he was okay, but he didnt have time to text back. What was on the computer screen was more important. Only one result showed up; a man that taught in Napia. *He teaches in Napia?* That's close. His thoughts quickly went to his age. *Wait, this guy is still teaching? He must be really old.* He knew he had to talk to him. Nevek had never been to the school in Napia, so it might be hard to find him. Then he remembered that he wasn't allowed to go to that school before. *Is this man the reason I couldn't go to this school?*

The idea intrigued him even more.

Next stop: Napia.

Endy hoped no one in the taproom noticed Zavier's erratic behavior, but she knew it was a false hope. He was a loud, obnoxious drunk.

He told her about how Nevek was chasing a dead end and wouldn't let this "Martian thing" go. He also told her about him banishing the Martians, but she didn't believe that part. She wanted to get a hold of Nevek, but she was busy trying to babysit her drunk boyfriend. She'd just have to ask later.

Just then, Dwerth walked in the door. Endy noticed him right away. *What's he doing here? Someone must have called the cops. Just great!*

Dwerth talked to the barkeeper briefly and walked over to Zavier, who had calmed down for the moment. It took a second, but he recognized him as he approached the table. "Well. Well. Well. I knew I'd run into you again."

"What do you want, Dwerth?" Endy snapped.

"Ah. Remember, it's *Officer* Dwerth to you. And I'm just doing my job." He put his hands in the air. "I'm here to pick up my good friend... Zavier, was it?"

"We don't want any trouble. We were just leaving." Endy gathered a few things and stood up.

"Oh, I just got here," Dwerth begged sarcastically with a chuckle. "But if you do have to leave, it'll be without your boyfriend. He'll be coming with me."

"I'm not going with nobody!" Zavier slurred.

"Come now. You don't want to keep your friends waiting."

"What do you mean?" Endy asked.

"Your Martian friends are in jail as we speak. They're getting ready to go before Chancellor Cassio." He cocked his head and stroked his chin. "Hmm. I wonder what they're gonna talk about."

Endy was stunned. *Is he telling the truth?* She could only watch as Dwerth took a staggering Zavier to the squad car and drove off.

CHAPTER 22

Two officers prepped the Martians for a meeting with the Chancellor. They shackled their hands and feet and led them out of the station like two inmates on death row.

We don't deserve this. Jerika looked over at Urial as they finished restraining him.

He could see she was worried. "Everything will be all right," he told her. His calm exterior didn't match the uncertainty he felt inside—he didn't know what to expect.

They got into a squad car and rode to the capital of the planet, Oxator, where Cassio's residence was. Jerika again looked over at Urial, who had his head down. *He must be praying.* She didn't interrupt him, but looked out the window the rest of the trip. Buildings and people went by. People going about their lives. So many people that needed to hear about Jesus. *How could this entire planet not have heard of him?*

"Lord, be with us now," she prayed quietly. "Help us to accept whatever comes to pass and return home safe." Her mind then went to Nevek. "And be with Nevek. Comfort him through this trying time. Help him to see who you are. I pray this in Jesus' name, amen."

The officer drove to the premises and walked Urial and Jerika up to the door. Surprisingly, there were no gates or outside wall. *I guess with all the security, they don't need them.* The mansion was an enormous, four-story structure. There were a lot of windows, which had to mean a lot of rooms. They knew they weren't there for a tour. Jerika noticed bystanders looking on with curiosity. She felt ashamed as she entered. Once inside, a couple of straight-faced bodyguards took over as escorts. They were more bulky and seemed to be in no hurry. The Martians had to slow their pace to accomodate them.

The two looked at the paintings and knickknacks down the corridor to Cassio's office. There were a couple of paintings that depicted the same man. Jerika thought it must be the Chancellor. She shuddered as one of the bodyguards opened the door. Cassio stood waiting for them, leaning on the front of his desk as they entered. "Well, hello," was all that came out of Cassio's mouth.

"Hello, sir," Urial answered.

Cassio was wearing a nice suit. They had similar ones on Mars for wealthier people. His black hair was slicked back and he had a cheesy smile on his face, just like the paintings.

Cassio wasn't sure what to think about the two people in front of him. They didn't look menacing. *Looks can be deceiving*, he reminded himself. "Come, please sit down." He walked toward his chair behind his desk and motioned for them to have a seat. "I've heard about you two and I just wanted to say, welcome to Ceres."

"I'm sorry, but can you take these off? They're not necessary." Jerika held up her hands, showing Cassio the restraints.

"Oh, those are just precautionary measures. I am the Chancellor of the planet," he gloated.

"We understand sir, but she's right. They're just not needed. We pose no threat to you or your planet. My name is Urial. My friend Jerika, here, came here by mistake. I only came here to bring her back home."

Jerika glared at Urial. *What is he doing?* Urial looked back at Jerika's expression. He nodded to her as if to say, "I'll handle this." She didn't like it, but she wanted to stay alive. Maybe cordial *was* the way to go about this.

Cassio looked back at his guests. "So, Mars is really another planet, huh?"

Jerika decided to answer this time. "Yes, and we just want to get home. Can you help us?"

"You're not just yanking my neck on this? You're really not from here?"

"Yes. I'm from a place called Trinion."

Urial added also, "And I'm from Hevah. Two cities on Mars, which we miss greatly."

They seemed believable, but Cassio just wanted to be sure. He leaned in, "So, you're not here to steal any classified information or try and take over our planet or something."

"What? No, sir," Jerika exclaimed. "We're Christians and don't believe in anything of that sort."

Urial looked over at his friend. He was hesitant to bring up their religion, but it was too late for that now. "Yes, we believe in doing good to others. Peace for all mankind, no matter what city...or planet they might come from. So, as we said earlier, these aren't necessary," holding up his restraints. "We're just looking to get back to our home planet."

Cassio leaned back in his chair. "Christians, huh? Never heard of it."

"Not many people here have," Jerika mumbled.

"Well, I'll tell you what I believe. I believe I'm a good person, so I'm gonna let you go."

"You will?" they both asked simultaneously.

"Yes, but only under one condition."

The two looked at each other. "Um...okay. What is it?" Urial inquired.

Cassio leaned forward again. "You get back into whatever it is you came here in, and you do not come back—ever."

Jerika was a bit taken aback. Even more so when Urial agreed to the conditions.

"Then we have a deal," he nodded. "GUARDS!" he yelled. The two jumped in their seats. Another guard peaked his head in. "Get the officers to take these restraints off and show our lovely guests the way out."

"Thank you, Chancellor."

"Please, call me Cassio," he laughed. "You'll never see me again anyway."

The two Martians looked at each other and smiled.

"Thank you, Cassio," Jerika said as an officer came in. He took the restraints off and escorted them out of the mansion. The two had never felt so free.

Nevek arrived at Rhybex Academy in Valtux as kids were scattered about. *Maybe it's some sort of break time.* He assumed that the best and easiest way to find Salem was to ask the front director.

Nevek made his way in and immediately saw the director. After a friendly greeting, he asked for the whereabouts of Salem. The director pointed Nevek to a classroom near the back of the building. He thanked him and went on his way.

Nevek glanced at young adults as he walked by. They didn't seem any different than him. Why should they? They're just like him. They just attended a different academy. He wasn't sure why he thought they'd be different. He received a couple of weird looks, but for the most part, he went unnoticed. They didn't seem too bothered by him.

Quicker than he'd anticipated, Nevek reached Salem's classroom. He wasn't sure what to expect. He hoped he was as friendly as the front director. He opened the door and walked inside.

The room was empty, except for an older gentleman sitting at his desk in the back. He didn't have much hair, but the few he did have were white like Nevek's. So was his groomed beard. He was deep in thought. *Probably writing the syllabus for the day.* Nevek didn't think he heard him come in. He cleare his throat. "Mr. Salem?" he asked.

The man looked up at Nevek. "Yes?"

Nevek started to get nervous. "Uh, my name is Nevek. I was wondering if I could ask you some things."

Figuring he was a student, Salem accepted.

Man, he must be really old. Nevek didn't want to get sidetracked. *Stay focused.* "Well, I was wondering if you could tell me about the Martian myth."

Salem's eyes widened in surprise. "The Martian myth? Wow. I haven't heard that in a long time. What class is teaching that?"

"Oh, no. I don't go to school here. I learned about it from my grandfather. Well…some of it. I was hoping you could fill me in on the rest."

"Huh. I didn't think anyone talked about Mars anymore." Salem put his netbook down. "What have you heard so far?"

"Well, like I said, not much. My grandfather didn't really seem like he wanted to talk about it." Just then, Nevek's telecom beeped. He wasn't interested in answering, so he just muted it. "Sorry."

"That's all right." Salem's interest was piqued. "So, what? Your grandfather told you to come talk to me?" he inquired.

"Well, no. He just kinda mentioned you..." Nevek trailed off. *Could this guy really help me?* He sighed. "Look, I'm sorry if I wasted your time." He turned around to leave.

"No, wait! I'm glad you asked. I just don't get asked about it that often is all."

Nevek stopped and faced the professor again. "So you know about Mars?"

"Yes. The *red planet*, as some call it."

Nevek sat down in a chair. "So, it's not like our planet?"

"Right. Each planet is a little different."

Nevek was confused. "Wait, there are more planets?"

It was now Salem's turn to be confused. He cocked his head. "Yes. You didn't know that?"

"No. They don't teach that in Napia. I assumed it was the same everywhere."

Salem shook his head. "Yeah, it's become a thing of the past, I'm afraid. It started as a cover-up by our government. We weren't allowed to tell anyone about it. Then, as time went on, people just forgot about it altogether. It got worse with each generation," he said. "I assume your grandfather didn't teach you either?"

"No, he got angry when I brought it up."

"Still angry, huh?" He paused. "You said he knew me. What's his name?"

"Ohkly."

"Ohkly?" Salem was beside himself. "Wow. I haven't heard that name in an even longer time. You're Ohkly's grandson? That's amazing." He laughed to himself.

"So, you were friends?"

"A *long* time ago."

"Why does he hate Martians so much?"

"Well, I'm assuming it's not all Martians. Just a certain few. These few had a weird belief that if you didn't believe like they did, they would do harm to you. Even kill you. This was when your grandfather was a young lad, but people like Ohkly didn't like it; and so there was this war waged amongst the Martians. While in this war, these people with the weird beliefs scanned our solar system and found that this planet, Ceres, looked like it could sustain life. And when they won the war, they banished the unbelievers to this planet where they were forced to live. They didn't expect the unbelievers to survive. When they found that we did, they just left us alone, never to speak to us again. I'm assuming that's why we call it a 'myth' today. We don't want anything to do with the people of the *red planet.*"

"Woah. So, it *is* real?"

Salem chuckled. "Yes, it is."

"Those weird believers sound like bad people."

"Well, some of them."

"They sound like Christians to me."

The statement hit Salem like a meteor. His interest spiked and eyes widened. He leaned forward in his chair. "How do you know about Christians?" he asked his young guest.

"I've encountered a couple. One crashed here and her friend came to rescue her. They tried to get me to believe too, but I didn't want any part of it. I told them to go back home."

Salem was delighted. "They tried to teach you about Jesus?"

Nevek was puzzled. "Yeah, that's him. The...'Messiah' ...right?"

"Yes, He paid the price for our sins on the planet Terra long, long, ago. Terra was actually where life started. The people back then crucified Jesus on a cross, but that was God's plan all along. So that we could be set free from our sins."

"Wait, crucified?"

"Yes. It was their way of killing bad people. Like our De-Ox vault today."

"Wait a minute. How do you know so much about Christians?"

Salem looked Nevek in the eye, "Because I am a Christian."

CHAPTER 23

Nevek was astounded. Speechless. He couldn't believe a Christian was living on Ceres this whole time. How had he never known? He then remembered that he wasn't allowed to attend this academy. His grandfather and father prevented him from coming here... probably to keep him from meeting Salem. *But wait. Didn't he just say that it was the Christians that drove out the unbelievers?*

"So, are you saying that Christians are the ones responsible for driving out those who didn't believe what they believed?"

"Sadly, yes. They professed to be Christians," Salem answered.

"So, my grandfather was just protecting me from you guys, huh?"

"Oh, no. No. I admit these were bad Christians. And that's what he's basing his prejudices on. Not all Christians are like them. I'm not like them. It's upsetting, but there are different 'Christians' out there."

"What does that mean? Isn't there only one type of Christian?"

"According to the Bible, yes. However, there are others that interpret it differently. If you interpret it wrong, you could draw false conclusions. This just creates a whole bunch of confusion and causes people to believe in false teachings."

Nevek stared blankly back at him. Salem could see this

was all new to the young man.

"Here, what are the Christians like that you met?"

"Uh...I don't know. They were nice people, I guess. They were kind and respectful."

"Exactly. That's what a Christian is supposed to be. They're loving to everyone. Jesus told us to love everyone as he loved us. I mean, he came to die for us. He says that's the ultimate kind of love. One that's willing to lay their life down for someone. Wouldn't you agree?"

Nevek sat there, trying to piece everything together. "Well, yeah." His thoughts then went to his father. "But what about Hell?

Salem looked confused. "They told you about Hell?"

"Well, technically, I asked them."

"Well, it's for the people who don't believe and trust in what God promised us. The gift of salvation." Salem tried to keep it vague.

"Those who don't serve him, right?"

"Yes, that is correct. See, when God created man back on Terra, they sinned against him. They didn't trust in what he said and so he cursed the planet. The whole universe really. That's why things die now. Because of our ancestors; the first man and woman ever created."

"He brought about death?"

"No, we did when we disobeyed him. Mankind rejects God all the time now and sins against him. They do wrong by him. It's only when we see that we've done wrong by him and need his help in this life that we are saved and don't go to Hell."

"Oh, okay. Well, my dad just died." Nevek dropped his head.

"I'm sorry to hear that."

"Do you think he's in Hell?"

Salem didn't know how to respond, but he had an idea. "Let me show you something," he said as he bent down. He came up and put a netbook on his desk. He turned it on and scrolled through a few things before motioning Nevek to join him. "This is the book of Luke in the Bible. Are you familiar with the Bible at all?"

"Yeah. A little."

"Okay, I'm in the sixteenth chapter. Here Jesus tells the story of a rich man who died and went to Hell. Just read from here," he pointed to the screen.

After a moment, Nevek said he finished.

"Okay, notice what this rich man did. He told Abraham to send this beggar back to Terra. Bring him back to life, so he could warn his brothers about this horrible place. This place of torment."

Nevek wasn't sure where he was going. "Okay, yeah."

"Well, I didn't know your father, but if he is in Hell, he's trying his hardest to get you to not go there with him. He wouldn't want you to end up there too."

The statement cut deep into Nevek. He was stunned. Again. He walked away from the desk. He had to sit down. *Is Salem right?*

"Look, son. I know it's a lot to take in. I don't believe anything happens by chance. I believe you're here for a reason. It's because there is a God and he wanted you here, this sol, learning about him. He wants everyone to come to a knowledge of him. Seek him out."

Nevek remembered the passage he first read from Jerika's Bible. *Was that the part he was talking about?* He wasn't sure if he could listen to anymore. He walked out as Salem was still talking. He had to get away. Anywhere.

Endy ran all the way to Arys' pod. Given her state of mind, she was surprised she remembered where it, was having only been there once. She felt it was the only place to go.

She ran up to the door and hit the chime. "Please be home. Please be home. Please be home..." she repeated to herself.

The door opened and she saw Arys standing there. Endy asked frantically, "Do you know where Nevek is?"

Arys wasn't too thrilled to have company at this time. "No, sorry."

Endy grunted.

"You're his friend from the discussion we had aren't you?"

"Yes, I am."

"Sorry. I don't think I got your name..." Arys trailed off as she motioned for her to enter.

"Endy."

"Right. No, I've been trying to get a hold of him too, with no luck. Not sure where he is," she said as she closed her door.

"Well, we've got a problem. Jerika and Urial have been arrested!" Endy exclaimed.

"Really? I was wondering why they weren't here."

"Yeah, it's gets worse," she continued. "I don't know if there was some kind of fight, but apparently Nevek told them to leave the planet. I'm assuming that when they went to leave is when they got arrested. They're going before the

Chancellor."

"The Chancellor? That doesn't sound good. Why the Chancellor?"

"No idea."

Something didn't sit right with Arys. "Wait. How do you know all of this?"

Endy tried to calm herself. "Zavier just got arrested and he told me about Nevek and then Dwerth told me about Jerika and Urial."

"Who's Dwerth?"

Endy was a little stumped. "Oh…sorry. The cop. He's had a few run-ins with Nevek."

"Oh, yeah. I knew that name sounded familiar. He was the one that got Nevek on stealing stuff at the hospital."

"Yes. Speaking of, I've got to find him to ask about his fight with Jerika. Why would he tell them to go home?"

"Yeah. That does sound odd. I'll try him again. Feel free to stay here until we find him."

Jerika and Urial headed out of the capital building. Neither knew what just happened, but thanked God for their freedom. "So, that was weird, right?" Urial said.

"Yeah, I don't understand it either," Jerika admitted.

"Well, it's behind us now. Let's just get back to Mars."

"Yeah, you're right." Jerika hung her head. Urial didn't notice at first, but caught a glimpse of it after a few moments. He put his arm around her and gave her a side hug.

"Everything will be okay. We'll be home soon."

"I know. It's just, I'm gonna miss this place."

Urial laughed. "Really? You weren't even here that long. You barely know anything about this planet."

"I know. It's a weird feeling. It has some good people on it though." Jerika thought about her friends. "Urial, we have to say goodbye before we leave."

"What? Are you insane? You heard the Chancellor. We have to go home. Now!"

"We are going home. He didn't say anything about not saying bye. It would be rude not to."

Urial gave her the look he gave her when she told him she was going to Ceres. A look of complete bewilderment.

"Come on. It won't take long. Then we'll be on our way."

"You heard how Nevek talked to us, right?"

Jerika hung her head again and turned the other way. "I know. I feel bad. It's mainly for the others though."

Urial rolled his eyes. "Fine, but please, let's hurry."

Jerika lifted her head and thanked her friend as they starting walking again. Her mind was still on Nevek. "I wish we could help Nevek somehow."

"We already did. You showed him the gospel. It's all in God's hands now."

"Yeah, I forget that part sometimes."

Urial looked around them. "So. Do you know where to go?"

"Yeah, I think I remember." They headed for a CUET station and journeyed back to Arys' dwelling.

CHAPTER 24

Ohkly had had enough. The vandalism was getting worse. He went to the planetary force station in Zand to get it resolved.

He walked as fast as his old body could up to the front desk. The secretary was on a call, so he had to wait. He looked around as officers and staff walked to and fro. Surprisingly, there wasn't much noise. He saw mostly cops typing away on their computers. *Must be hard at work. Not like the ones in Elvers.* He then felt glad he didn't have to work anymore. After a few moments, the secretary hung up her telecom and asked Ohkly how she could help.

"I would like to speak to the Chief of the planetary force. I'm trying to get someone down to catch these vandals near my home."

"He's actually busy at the moment. Can I take a message?"

Ohkly got agitated. "No. I'll wait, dear. Thank you," he said through grittrf teeth.

He didn't know where to go, so he leadned against the wall. He noticed a young man in restraints. Ohkly wasn't a shy person at all. "It'll be all right," he said to the prisoner.

The kid looked up to see who was talking. "Thanks, old man," he snarled, as he put his head back down.

"You better respect your elders, boy," Ohkly snapped back respectfully.

The young man looked back up. "Just leave me alone."

Ohkly squinted at the young man. "Hey, do I know

you? Weren't you at my son's funeral?"

The young man inspected Ohkly. "Yeah, I remember you. You're Nevek's grandfather, right?"

"Oh, yes sir. Ohkly's the name."

"Zavier."

"Well, what are you doing here?"

"Apparently, I was disturbing the peace," Zavier replied waving his hands in the air. "It's all Nevek's fault. He's too involved with these Martians."

Ohkly cocked his head. "Did you say *Martians*? You know about them too?"

"Yeah. He's become friends with them. I say they're up to no good. They've gotten in his head."

Ohkly became a little irritated. "He told me he wasn't seeing them anymore, that he made them leave."

"Well, he did. It's just...he just keeps trying to figure them out. I told him to just leave them alone."

"Yep. That's what I told him too. I don't know what to do with him."

"I don't either. Word around here though is that they got arrested."

"Who? The Martians?"

"Yeah. That's what I heard. Can't confirm it though."

"Really? That'd be good news. Keep 'em locked up." Ohkly stuck his chest out.

Zavier looked at him a little funny. "You don't like Martians, do you?"

"No, son, I don't."

The receptionist interrupted and told Ohkly that the Chief was ready to see him now. He told Zavier to enjoy his day and walked into Chief Haros' office. Haros was looking at his netbook when he entered. He finished with up with it and asked how he could help.

"Well, I was going to ask you about my neighborhood being vandalized, but I heard something more important is going on."

Haros leaned back his chair. "Oh, yeah. What's that?"

"I heard from a little birdy that you have some Martians locked up?"

Haros became suspicious. "Yes, sir. May I ask how you know that?"

"Eh, people are talking," Ohkly brushed it off.

"Yeah...well...let's keep this our little secret," Haros said as he pointed to the two of them.

"Fine by me. If it was up to me though, I'd let them rot in there."

Haros was confused. "What do you mean?"

"You've never heard of the *Martian myth*?"

"Sure. We all have, haven't we?"

"Well, it's died down since your time, but it's no myth." Ohkly preceded to tell Haros everything. That it was the Martians who forced the now-Cerean people here. That this planet wasn't inhabited until the 'Messianics' banished them to this deserted planet, and had no intent on having contact with them. The whole story. As Ohkly was talking, Haros' childhood memories came back to him. He remembered the things his parents told him. This got him furious.

Ohkly could see Haros tensing up in anger. His fists were clenched. His teeth were grinding. It was subtle, but Ohkly noticed. All he could do was smile. Just then, Haros' telecom went off. It was Chancellor Cassio. "Excuse me sir. It's the Chancellor. I have to take this."

Ohkly nodded. He turned around and headed out as Haros picked up the call. He wasn't very fast at his old age, so he had no problem hearing Haros scream at Cassio, "Why did you let them go!?"

Ohkly turned back around to listen in. He was shocked. It didn't take a genius to figure out that he was talking about the Martians.

Haros apologized for yelling at Cassio and had to explain why. He told him the whole story he had just received from Ohkly. About how the Cerean civilization came to be. After a few moments, and some nods, he said, "Yes, sir," a couple of times and then hung up. He slammed his telecom onto his desk in disgust. "We've got to find those Martians," he grunted.

Ohkly stood there in awe, trying to remain calm. "He had the Martians and he let them go?"

"Yep. He didn't see any fault in them, so he just let them go." Haros smiled. "But that all changed once I told him the truth."

"Those people are dangerous, Chief. If they haven't left yet, they need to be locked up. Or worse!"

Haros could see Ohkly's rage building. "It'll be okay, sir," he said with his hands out trying to calm him down as he stood up. "We'll find this plague to our planet and exterminate it." He put his hands on his desk and hung his head. "I wish I knew where they would've gone."

Ohkly had an idea. He looked out to see Zavier, but he wasn't sitting where he was earlier. They'd probably taken him to a holding cell. "Chief, I have an idea on where to find them. I'm sure he'll tell us everything."

"Let's do it!" Haros walked out of his office. "Dwerth, Talbot, we gotta move. Let's split up. We're going Martian hunting."

CHAPTER 25

Endy and Arys sat quietly, trying to figure out where Nevek, Jerika, and Urial were. After brainstorming for about half an hour, neither could think of anything. Arys asked about Zavier, but immediately regretted it when she remembered Endy said he got arrested. The door chime broke the silence, causing both of them to jump. They both rushed to the door, hoping one of their missing friends would be standing there. Arys got to the door first and opened it.

"Told you I knew how to get back," Jerika joked to Urial.

Endy lunged at Jerika and gave her a hug. "I'm so glad you're okay."

"Yeah, why wouldn't we be?" Jerika asked.

"We heard you got arrested."

"Yeah, that was a little scary, but God brought us through it."

"So, what happened?" Arys asked.

"Yeah, did Nevek really tell you to leave?" Endy wondered.

The question took the Martians by surprise. All they could do was give a nervous chuckle. "Yeah, he did," Urial answered. "And on our way back to the ship, the officer got us. I must admit, it was a little frightening."

Jerika spoke up. "I don't even know how long we were in the cell, but it felt like forever. Then we went before your ruler. A chancellor?"

"You went before Chancellor Cassio?" Arys inquired.

"Yeah. He didn't seem too happy we were here," Urial explained. "We had to tell him that we come in peace and weren't here to do anyone harm. We just wanted to get back home. After a small talk, he let us go, but only if we agreed to leave immediately; which we were going to, but Jerika insisted we say goodbye first."

"Oh, that was nice of you," Endy said.

"Yeah, so we gotta get going. Is Nevek here?" Jerika asked.

"No, we've been trying to get a hold of him, but no luck," Arys answered. "I'm sorry he told you guys to leave. That doesn't sound like him. If he were here, I'd make him apologize."

"Oh. No, that's okay," Jerika said. "He was just angry at the time. You guys have been through a lot. Not a big deal. Just tell him and the others we said bye, okay?"

"Yes, and thank you for taking care of Jerika," Urial said. "Because of you, she is alive."

"Hey, not a problem," Arys replied. "Just helping out where we can."

"It was lovely to meet you all. I'm just glad not many people know we're here. It'll be easier to sneak out," Urial laughed a little.

Just then, Arys and Endy's telecoms went off. They both read their messages. "Uh, you might want to take that back," Arys said with fear in her eyes. "We just got an alert that says you guys escaped from jail." She showed them her telecom. "Now the whole planet knows you're here."

Nevek had a lot on his mind as he got off the CUET.

Salem's words cut like a dagger to the heart. He knew he had to apologize to Urial and Jerika. *Please don't be gone yet.* He didn't want his anger to be the last thing they saw of him. He ran, hoping against rationality that they hadn't left yet.

Night was approaching as he made it to Napia, where Jerika's ship had crashed. He passed Sprokutt's, where he and Zavier had been that night. It was busy. *Maybe there's an event going on.* He wasn't interested though.

Nevek jogged down the street where he thought he had gone. He tried to remember the scenery and things around him, but it was fuzzy. He spun around, scanning the area to see if anything could jog his memory, but nothing did. After a few steps, he realized he was walking back towards the tram station. *Makes sense... that's where I would have headed.*

Nevek began looking around again to remember what he was doing that night. He remembered looking up at a shooting star. The star that turned out to be a spacecraft. He looked up, imagining a star flying across the sky and he followed it down to the ground in the distance. There was an opening. It lead to an uninhabited field. *That has to be it.*

Nevek walked quickly, then broke into a full run toward an uninhabited part of the planet. The farther he went, the quieter it got. The only noise was the wind blowing past his ears.

Then he saw it.

Jerika's ship; or the pile of battered metal that *was* her ship. He searched around for clues, but quickly realized that it wouldn't tell him anything he wanted to know.

Nevek scanned the surrounding area, but didn't see

much. He turned behind him and saw something else in the distance. He ran to it, knowing already what it was. *Urial's ship!* He was relieved. *Wait! But, that would mean they're still here. What are they still be doing here?* He took out his telecom, but before he could check it, he heard a noise.

"Well, well, well. Looks like third times a charm," Dwerth remarked.

CHAPTER 26

"I don't even know what to say," Jerika said. "That's not true."

"Right. The Chancellor let us go," Urial added, nervously.

Endy turned to Arys. "Okay, well, what do we do?"

Arys shrugged. "I don't know."

"We have to get back to my ship and leave at once," Urial stressed.

"Right," Jerika said. They turned to walk out. She grabbed Urial's hand. "Wait a minute. What if they're waiting for us by the ship like last time?"

"Oh, you're right. They know where the ship is. We need a place to hide out for a while."

"You can stay here," Endy suggested.

"Could the police find us here?"

"I don't think so."

"Well, we'll have to stay then. We gotta think of a plan though."

"Good thinking," Jerika uttered.

The chime went off and the four of them looked at each other nervously. Arys was frightened to open the door, so she used the peep-cam on the outer part of the door to screen who it was. "Isn't that Nevek's friend?"

Endy jumped up and looked. "Yeah, that's Zavier." She opened the door for him. "Zave, what are you doing here."

Zavier peeked inside as if to scope out the place. "I'm here to break up with you." He then leaned back and yelled,

"Yeah, they're in here!" Endy stared at him as her jaw dropped.

Arys looked on the peep-cam monitor as two police officers walked down the hallway and stood next to Zavier. "Well done, kid," Haros said to him.

Almost impulsely, Endy went to shut the door, but Talbot stuck his foot in the way. "Not so fast," he said. "It's rude not to invite us in." Endy backed away in fear.

"Zavier, what's going on?" Jerika asked.

"They told me you escaped from jail, so I had to tell them where you'd be," he explained.

"You know that's not true!" Urial exclaimed

"Sorry, Chancellor's orders," Talbot said.

"What is wrong with you?" Endy asked in anger. She walked up to Zavier and slapped him on the cheek. Zavier glared at her, then the corners of his mouth raised up into an evil smile and he shoved her hard, causing her to fall to the floor. Arys went to her aid. Talbot restrained him from doing anything more. He sent him outside while the police did their job.

"Okay, Urial. Let's go…again," Talbot said snarkily.

"I'm not going with you."

"Don't make us do this the hard way, son," Haros said. He grabbed at Jerika's arm, but Urial quickly stepped in between them

"Like I said, we're not going back to jail. We haven't done anything wrong here," he said.

Haros laughed. "Oh, you're not going back to jail."

"Then, where are you taking them?" asked Endy.

"They're going to the vault."

Endy covered her mouth in shock. Arys was speechless

as well. Unbeknownst to the Martians, the DE-OX vault was the planet's form of the death penalty. The victim is put into a chamber where the oxygen is removed and the person dies from asphyxiation. Though it didn't happen very often, anyone caught escaping jail was automatically sentenced to the vault.

A small tremor knocked most of them off balance. Urial fell into the wall and hit his head. Talbot, one of the few who remained upright in the asteroid-enduced earthquake, took gleeful notice of Urial's plight, and took full advantage of it, grabbing the suspects and restraining them.

Haros pulled out his gun and aimed it at Arys and Endy. "Don't try anything foolish, ladies." His gloating tone did nothing to endear him to the girls, but the weapon convinced them that they shouldn't interfere."

Endy turned away and started to cry. Arys felt powerless. *What can we do?* She watched silently as her friends walked, handcuffed, down the hallway, and out towards the squad car.

"What...what are you doing here?" Nevek asked.

"Just trying to catch some scum," Dwerth replied.

"What do you mean?"

"You mean, you don't know? Your alien friends are wanted. The whole planet is looking for them."

Nevek's eyes grew wide as he almost fell backwards. "What?"

"And you're gonna help me find them."

"But...I...I don't know where they are."

Dwerth laughed. "Oh, come on, boy. Don't play stupid. We both know you're just covering your rear end."

"No...really Dwerth. I don't know where they are. Last time I talked to them, they were on their way home. Here, let me just check." Nevek pulled out his telecom and didn't even get the screen on before it was knocked out of his hand and landed near Urial's ship. He looked up just in time to see Dwerth's fist. The blow knocked him on his buttocks. He was dazed for a moment, but Dwerth quickly came back into vision as he rubbed his sore cheek.

Dwerth bent over and grabbed him by the collar of his suit. "Listen, Nevek. I don't have time for your games. Just tell me where they are or I'm taking you in for aiding criminals who escaped from jail."

"Escaped? They're Christians. They wouldn't escape from jail."

"Hey, I just go by what they tell me."

Nevek picked up some dirt and threw it in Dwerth's eyes, causing him to release his grip. He jumped up and started to run away. He got a few steps and remembered his telecom. He turned back and ran to the spacecraft. The telecom was laying face-down in the dirt, just a few feet from the edge of the ship. He bent over as he ran and picked it up in stride, only to be pushed into the ship. He hit his shoulder hard and cried out in pain. Dwerth picked him up and squeezed his hand around Nevek's throat. Immediately, Nevek kneed Dwerth in the stomach, freeing him again from the officer's grasp. Free, Nevek attempted to run away again, putting his telecom in his pocket.

He had only taken a few steps when an asteroid collided into the planet not too far from them. The gound rumbled and quaked beneath them, knocking both men off their feet. Nevek landed in some dirt while Dwerth fell into the ship, hitting his head. Nevek got up and ran for all he was worth, not even bothering to look back. The only thing on his mind was getting back to Arys'. He got to the CUET station and hopped on the tram. He finally was able to check his telecom and used it to call his sister.

Arys answered quickly. "Where have you been?"

"Look, I don't have time. I'll be there soon. I think the police are after Urial and Jerika."

"Yeah. They were just here and took them. Your friend Zavier spilled everything to the police."

"What?" Nevek didn't have any other words. *What is Zavier doing?*

"Yeah, he came by and the police got them. They said it was the Chancellor's orders to have them killed. They're going to the DE-OX vault."

More bad news. Nevek wasn't in the mood to be hearing this. *This is all my fault.* He made up his mind to help out somehow, someway.

Little did he know that Dwerth had already informed Chief Haros to be on the lookout for him and that he might be headed his way.

Talbot put the prisoners into the back seat of the police car as Haros got off his telecom. "It was Dwerth," the Chief said, answering Talbot's unspoken question. "That white-haired troublemaker, Nevek, is probably heading this way right now."

Talbot grinned at the news.

"I'm going to go back inside and have another little chat with his sister." The Chief started up the walk towards the pods when Talbot stopped him.

"Hey, I thought of something, Chief." Haros turned around and looked at him. "I was thinking, instead of killing them both, maybe we only kill the girl and just rough up the guy."

"And why would we do a stupid thing like that?"

"Well, we can send him back to wherever he came from and tell them we're a force to be reckoned with. You know, give them a warning."

Haros just laughed as he walked back into the complex. "You are an idiot, son. Just stay here. I'll be right back."

Talbot stood there, silently steaming inside. He thought it was a good idea. He turned around to the sound of someone laughing. He opened the door and dragged Urial out and threw him to the ground. "You think that's funny?" Talbot kicked him in ribs a couple of times and mocked him while he was on the ground.

"Stop it!" Jerika shouted from the car. Talbot just ignored her. Urial grunted in pain as the officer picked him up and threw him up against the car. He hurled his fist at Urial's face, cutting him above the eyebrow. He set him up again and landed another one, cutting the inside of his cheek.

Urial struggled to regain his balance, unable to use his hands, which were cuffed behind him. "I've not done anything wrong," he muttered through the pain.

Jerika yelled again. "Stop it! He wasn't laughing!"

Talbot kneed Urial in the stomach, almost knocking the wind out of him. He watched as Urial fell to the ground with a *thud*.

Chief Haros ran to the car, cursing at Talbot. "What do you think you're doing, Officer?"

"Sorry sir, I don't know what came over me," he said as he tried to catch his breath.

Haros looked him dead in the eye. "You're a disgrace to the department. Give me your badge. You're off this force!"

"But Chief, I…"

"Now!"

Talbot pulled out his badge and gun and placed them in Haros' open hand. The now-former officer hung his head. Haros took Talbot's gun and whacked him in the back of the head, sending him to his knees. Talbot's head spun, but heard Haros pick up Urial and get in his car and drive off.

Nevek slammed his head in frustration on the tram wall after reading the texts from his sister. Great, now they're looking for me too, and Arys' place is being watched. Then his telecom buzzed again with a text from Sqett. "HEY. ARE YOU WITH JERIKA? I HAD SOME MORE QUESTIONS. ALSO YOU HAVE BEEN TRUANT FROM CLASS BUT I KNOW YOUR MIND ISN'T CLEAR. JUST WONDERING IF ALL IS WELL. TAKE CARE."

Nevek rolled his eyes and sighed. School was the last thing on his mind. He wasn't even sure if he'd ever go back. Then a lightbulb went off. *Wait, that's it! School.* He figured that would be the safest place for him at the moment. He texted Sqett the coordinates to the academy in Napia and told him to meet him there. He had to go back and talk to Salem.

Dwerth made his way back to Arys' pod. As he pulled

up he saw Talbot sitting at the entrance to the building, looking glum. "What are you doing out here?" he asked.

"I messed up, sir."

Dwerth got a little worried. "What do you mean? Did you get the Martians?"

"Yes."

Dwerth let out a sigh of relief. "Well, thanks for telling me!"

"Oh, sorry. I didn't know."

"Right. So, what do you mean you messed up?"

"I got a little angry and beat up one of the Martians, Urial. I just lost it. I don't know what came over me. Chief fired me." Talbot lowered his head again.

Dwerth looked around. "Oh. So, he took them?"

"Yeah... Sir, I'll do anything to get my job back, please."

Dwerth looked over at Arys' pod. "Do they know you've been fired?" He asked as he pointed.

"No, I don't think so," Talbot said as he looked back.

Dwerth removed his badge and handed it to Talbot. "I can't get your job back, but I do need your help. Let's go."

CHAPTER 27

Nevek got off in Valtux and remembered exactly where to go. He ran most of the way, still trying not to be seen. He reached the school and headed up the stairs to the front door when he heard Sqett. "Nevek, you brought me to another academy? Is this where Urial and Jerika are?"

Nevek turned around and grabbed him, pulling him into the building.

"Where are we headed?" Sqett asked.

Nevek tried to fill him in. "Urial and Jerika have been arrested and I'm trying to figure out how to get them free. In the meantime, I know someone who may have answers to your questions."

"Who?"

They reached Salem's classroom. They opened the door to find Salem packing up some stuff. *He must have just finished up a session.*

Salem looked up at them and smiled. "Ah, back so soon? And you brought a friend, I see."

"I need a place to stay for a while and this seemed like a good place," Nevek said cheekily.

"Well, I'm getting ready to leave. Why don't you come to my house?"

"No, I can't. I'd like to just stay here, if that's okay. My friend has some questions too."

"Oh?"

"Hello sir. My name is Sqett," he introduced.

"Salem. Nice to meet you."

Sqett looked at Nevek. "How is he going to assist me with my questions?"

Nevek smiled at Salem. "Salem here is a Christian too."

"What?"

"Yeah. Look, Urial and Jerika have been arrested and I have to find a way to free them," Nevek explained. "In the meantime, Salem can help you."

"Wait. Why have your friends been arrested?" Salem inquired.

"The authorities found out about them. I'm not sure how, but my friend Zavier had something to do with it."

"Zavier got them arrested?" Sqett asked incredulously.

"Yeah, I don't think he's on our side anymore."

"We have to get them out of there," Salem said.

"I know. I'll think of something," Nevek responded.

Salem was both worried about his Christian brethren, and excited about someone showing interest in his faith. He set his things down and turned to Sqett. "So, you had some questions? How can I help you?"

Nevek took a seat near the back, trying to listen, but focusing more on trying to save his friends. Sqett pulled out his netbook and showed it to Salem. "Well, I have been reading your book..."

Salem interrupted with a laugh, "It's not my book, son. It's God's book, but go on."

"Um...right...well as I was reading, I observed that near the beginning, God destroyed a lot of people. Nations even. And am I right in saying the whole world once?"

"Yes, that is correct. That was 'the Great Flood'. It covered the entire world of Terra. I assume that's where it got all of its water."

Sqett thought for a minute. "I remember Jerika saying that this God is loving? How is that loving?"

"I've gotten this question plenty of times. I'm not sure if you saw, but the Bible is divided into two parts: the old and new testaments. The Old Testament deals more with God's holiness. He hates when we sin. Habakkuk one-thirteen says that he can't even look at it, his eyes are too pure. *He* is too pure. So, we have to take that into consideration. We need to ask, 'Why did God destroy these people?' It was because of their wickedness. See, he is the giver of lifeand he can also take it away." Sqett sat quietly, processing his words. "Now the New Testament shows us his love. John three-sixteen says that he loves all mankind so much that he sent his Son to die in our place, sacrificing himself. We are sinful people, but God doesn't want us to remain sinful. He wants us to receive the gift of his Son that we might be forgiven of our sins. We don't have to bear the guilt of them any longer. God will wash us clean of them, never to remember them anymore."

This was all still new to the young men, so they struggled to grasp the reality of it. Nevek was still trying to compose a plan to free his friends, but quietly listening to Salem too. He was actually surprised that he could accomplish both at the same time.

Sqett remembered his earlier talks with the Martians. "I don't believe I have many, but, how do I have my sins forgiven?" asked Sqett.

"Great question. The Bible says to repent and be baptized." Salem quickly realized by the confused look on Sqett's face that he had no idea what that meant, so he elaborated. "To repent means to turn away from your old self. Not to desire things that *you* want, but what *God* wants. And baptism means to be immersed in water. This is re-enacting the death, burial, and resurrection of Jesus Christ, the Son of God. We *die* to our old self. We are *buried* in the water. Then we are *resurrected* to a new life in Christ. Freed from our past sins."

Nevek found himself leaning forward on the desk, taking in every word that Salem spoke to Sqett. His telecom went off though, disrupting his focus. Arys' message asked him to come to her place. His brows lowered in confusion as he re-read the text. He responded, "I THOUGHT YOU TOLD ME TO STAY AWAY FROM THERE."

After a few moments, she replied, "THE COAST IS CLEAR."

The coast is clear? That doesn't sound like Arys, but if she needs me, I have to go. Nevek got up and headed for the door. Salem looked up and asked where he was going. "Uh, my sister texted me. I think she needs my help. We're gonna figure out how to get our friends out."

Just then, their telecoms received an alert. It was delivered by the Chancellor himself:

"TWO CHRISTIANS HAVE TRESPASSED ON OUR PLANET AND ARE BEING SENTENCED TO DEATH. ANY OTHERS WILL BE TOO."

CHAPTER 28

Nevek's eyes widened as he read. They can't go to the vault. They didn't do anything wrong.

"We have got to do something, Nevek," Sqett said.

Nevek looked up from his phone. He didn't know what to say.

"Salem, how can we help our friends?" Sqett started to panic too.

"I don't know. Nothing like this has ever happened before." Salem sat in disbelief.

"Why do they want to kill Jerika and Urial?" Sqett asked aloud.

"He knows," Nevek said of Salem. "You have to help them. You know the truth. The truth can set them free," Nevek said as he walked back towards the other two. His mind then went back to the very first Bible verse he ever read. *The truth shall set you free. Is that it?* He wasn't sure.

"Me? I can't help them. They'd just kill me too, if I told them I was a Christian."

"Argh! Sqett, he'll fill you in on what's going on. I have to go. My sister and I will figure something out," Nevek said as he ran out. He wondered what Arys had to say in all of this.

Nevek made his way back to the Oxator station. Arys' pod wasn't far from it. He couldn't stop thinking about his friends as he wandered down the road. The friends who were about to be killed. *Think, Nevek. Think. There has to be a way to free them.*

Nevek approached the complex as night fell. The lights illuminated the sky. He was lost in thought when he heard a voice say "Hey!" right before someone shoved to the ground, his shoulder breaking his fall. After wincing in pain, he looked up at his attacker.

"Zavier, what are you doing?" he said as he tried to get up. He got to his knees as Zavier kicked him in the stomach.

"You just couldn't let this go, could you? You had to get me and all your friends involved in this stupid Martian drama," Zavier said as he glared menacingly.

"What do you mean? I was just trying to help them. To help Jerika."

"*Help Jerika!* You think getting her and her friend killed is helping them? You really are dumb, Nev."

"Zavier, where is this coming from?" Nevek said as he finally got up.

"I thought you had a thing for Jerika, but I know you and Endy have been hanging out a lot too. I never thought my best friend would try to take my girl, but maybe I was wrong."

Nevek put his hands up, "Zave, you know I wouldn't do that. It was one tiny kiss." He regretted the words as soon as they escaped his mouth.

"Kiss?"

"Crape," Nevek said to himself.

"You kissed her? So, there *is* a thing between you two?" Zavier charged.

"Wait Zave, no…" Nevek fell backwards as his best friend, or the one who had been his best friend, tackled him. As he landed on the ground, his head exploded in pain as Zavier began to pummel him with his fists. Zavier went for another swing, but Nevek was able to get his hand up to block it. He tried his other hand, but Nevek got both hands up to divert the punch and push Zavier off of him.

"Zavier, it was a mistake. I'm sorry. It shouldn't have happened," he said, backing up with his hands in defense mode.

Without a word, Zavier charged again. Nevek dodged to the right and pushed him as he went by, knocking him slightly off-balance.

"Zave, I don't want to fight you!" Nevek said sternly.

"Good. It will be easy for me to win," he said as he gave his friend a side kick to the ribs. It knocked Nevek back. Zavier quickly took advantage of the opening and connected with a right hand. Nevek fell on his backside. He was able to steady himself enough to keep his head from hitting too.

Zavier walked over and pushed Nevek down with his foot. "Consider this friendship over, buddy." He straddled Nevek and cocked back for one last punch, as a loud *crack* filled the air. Zavier yelled in pain as he crouched over. He slid off Nevek and grunted in agony on the ground.

Trying to catch his breath, Nevek looked up to see a gun, smoke rising from the barrel.

And holding the gun was Dwerth.

CHAPTER 29

Nevek went over to check on Zavier who was laying on the ground, screaming, and holding his left shoulder, as drops of blood began to fall. Being shot was a new and painful experience. Nevek looked up as Dwerth and Talbot drew closer walking towards them.

"I don't need you messing with my arrest, son," Dwerth said to Zavier.

"So you shot him!?" Nevek exclaimed.

"Had to get him off of you somehow. It's not like I killed him." Dwerth holstered his gun and picked up Nevek, who was too tired to put up a fight. "Let's go, Nevek."

Arys and Endy came running from the building to see what was going on. Endy yelled for Zavier and started towards him, but Dwerth put up his hand to stop her.

"Talbot, let's go. I'll take you home." Dwerth motioned his head in the direction of his car.

"What about him?" Talbot asked, pointing to Zavier on the ground.

Dwerth's telecom went off. As he answered it, he looked at Zavier. "Leave him." He turned and walked away to take his call. Talbot looked up at the girls, but went with Dwerth, who hung up his telecom.

"You can't just take him to jail!" yelled Arys.

Dwerth looked back at her. "Well, I was going to take him there, but I gotta make a stop first." He looked at Nevek. "And give me your telecom. Won't make that mistake again." Nevek handed it over as he was escorted by the policemen to the car.

Arys and Endy looked on helplessly as they drove off.

"What did he mean by that?" Endy asked.

"I don't know, but you have to get him to a hospital," Arys pointed at Zavier. "I'll follow Nevek."

"Where are you taking me?" Nevek asked.

"Well, we're not celebrating the fifteenth anniversary yet, but a good festivity would be to watch your friends die, no?" Dwerth said snarkily.

"What!? That's how we're going to 'celebrate'?"

"Sorry Nevek. Just doing my job. The Chief told me that's what the Chancellor wants."

"They don't deserve that. They're Christians. They're good people. I'm telling you, they wouldn't escape from jail."

Dwerth came to a red light and turned around to Nevek. "Now who am I supposed to believe: the Chancellor or some people from a planet we've never heard of until a few sols ago?"

Both Talbot and Nevek looked at Dwerth funny. Nevek really didn't have much to say, so he just leaned back in the seat, too exhausted to do anything else. Dwerth dropped Talbot off at his home, and then drove off again.

They pulled up to the Oxator prison, where the executions were going to take place. They were made to be a spectacle for public viewers as a way to teach them how not to behave. With this, the fifteenth anniversary, many were bound to be watching.

Nevek's nerves were out of control. *I don't deserve to be here. Jerika and Urial don't deserve to be in this situation either.* He closed his eyes. He could only think of one possibility.

Nevek didn't know what to say, or how to say it, so he just talked. "God, they need your help. Please help them. Help them make it out alive today." He couldn't explain it, but he felt a bit of calmness after he said those words.

Dwerth parked the car and turned around to face Nevek. "What did you say?"

"Oh...I was just praying."

"Praying?"

"Yeah. It's like talking to God."

Dwerth snickered. "God?" He looked around. "What's god?"

Nevek shook his head. "Never mind. It's complicated."

Dwerth got out of the car and opened Nevek's door. "Well, let's get going. We don't want to miss the big show."

Nevek felt the urge to fight back, but was having an equally powerful feeling that maybe he was supposed to be here. So, with Dwerth by his side, he walked up to the prison.

Just like any prison, there usually wasn't much excitement in the air. It was usually dark and gloomy, especially at night. However, this night was different. Monitors were on all over the complex, showing the prison officials setting up the DE-OX vault. This was going to a televised event. The Chancellor wanted to show the citizens that Ceres wasn't going to be messed with.

Crowds began walking into the prison complex, each

hoping to see the execution up close. *Don't they realize that innocent people are about to die?* He pondered that thought for a moment. *Of course, they don't. They've painted them as enemies of Ceres.* The vault was near the rear, so they had some walking to do.

Nevek remained quiet for the long walk, trying to come up with a plan to get out of there with his friends—without dying in the process. Nothing. *Maybe someone else is devising a plan too. Maybe not.*

They had taken a hidden path, away from all the people. Down long hallways of almost pure darkness. The cells looked like they hadn't been used in a long time. Dwerth seemed to know where he was going though. They finally entered the room where the show would be take place. The puffy eyes and red face told Nevek that Jerika had been crying. Urial, Nevek noticed, was bruised and had spots of dried blood on his face. *That's never a good sign.* Nevek felt pain in his heart over seeing them in this condition. He wanted to break his restraints, overpower Dwerth, and whisk his friends to safety. But, even in that unlikely scenario, there was still Chief Haros to contend with. He was sitting by the two prisoners, his gun very conspicuous on his hip. If Nevek thought they could hear him, he would have said that everything was going to be okay. But, he had a hard time convincing himself of that

Chancellor Cassio was talking to some bigwigs. A podium was fitted for microphones, and cameras were ready to roll. Dwerth found a spot near the back, so he guided Nevek and practically pushed him into a chair. After a few moments, Cassio went up to the podium to commence the festivities.

"My fellow Cereans. We gather together in celebration of our fifteenth anniversary as a civilization on this planet. We have accomplished much in that time. Unfortunately, what many of you don't know is the origin of how this planet came to be. I was informed about it recently and didn't want to believe it myself, so I did some of my own research. I've found that it is true and that it was intentionally being hidden from us by our government. Well, today I will uncover what was once covered, and reveal what I have found. Many people lost their lives in a struggle that led to them being banned from another planet. That planet is the closest one to us, called Mars. And I just so happen to have here, with me, two Martians. Back then, there was a group of people on that planet, who called themselves 'Christians.' They believed that those who didn't adopt their teachings didn't belong in their civilization. That they weren't welcomed in their communities. So they ended up shipping them to this planet. The one we stand on now; Ceres. That is how this society started. I don't know if the Christians know it or not, but we're still standing today, fifteen Cerean years later. Still going strong. Sure, we have those who paved the way for us, and for that we are grateful. We are here today, at the vault, because these two Martians in custody are in fact Christians."

The people gasped.

"Yes, yes, I know. But today, we shall let their planet know that we are a force to be reckoned with. Today, I have sentenced these two to the vault. Mars shall know not to send any more people here to Ceres. We are happy as our own society, and we will not be imposed on by outsiders. These two shall pay for the sins of their fathers and for the lives lost in the tragedy. So, without further ado; let the celebration begin!"

The crowds clapped and cheered for their leader. Nevek watched Urial give Jerika a hug for comfort. He couldn't believe the masses were actually in favor of this. *How could they be excited to watch two innocent people die?*

The policemen prepped the two prisoners. They took off the restraints and put them in front of the vault. Cassio got back onto the mic and rhetorically asked, "Ladies first?" The crowds cheered again, so the guards brought Jerika up to the clear, eight-foot cube.

Nevek watched as they opened the door to the death chamber. Jerika didn't move as they instructed her to go inside. She turned to the guards and pleaded with them not to go through with it. Instead, they pushed her in. She began crying as she fell to the floor, reaching back for someone to save her. Cassio quieted the crowd in order to get the full effect of the ambiance around them. They shut the door and all that could be heard were the faint cries for help coming from inside the vault. A guard then went over to the controls to prepare the execution process.

That's when a voice yelled from the crowd, "Wait!"

CHAPTER 30

Everyone was in awe as they turned to look a hand-cuffed, white-haired kid. "What are you doing?" Dwerth whispered to Nevek. Other whispers began to fill the room as they all stared at the young man. Urial was even more shocked, especially when he saw who shouted.

The Chancellor got on the microphone again. "Yes. Do you have an objection?"

"Yes, I do. These two did nothing wrong. They don't deserve to be sentenced to this."

Cassio squinted at him. "And who might you be, son?"

Dwerth sat Nevek down. "Okay, kid. That's enough." He tried to do it calmly.

As soon as Nevek's butt hit the chair though, he stood right back up, addressing Cassio. "My name is Nevek. I've had the privilege to meet those Martians and I don't believe they escaped from jail as you said they did."

Cassio chuckled. "I don't think that this up for debate. This decision cannot be disputed."

A lot of people looked back at Nevek, waiting to see if he'd respond.

A small murmur of complaints spread throughout some of the crowd as Arys, who had followed Dwerth to the prison, made her way toward the source of the commotion.

Nevek continued, "I was the one who housed these Martians. I take full responsibility for my actions and request I take the place of these two."

People began to murmur again. Arys looked on in fear. Cassio was confused as well. "I'm sorry, that's not possible. Like I said, this isn't up for debate. Sit down or I'll have you removed. Guard," he motioned for the guards to continue the process.

"No! Stop!" Arys shouted.

The guard again turned away from the controls. Everyone looked over to see who yelled, but Nevek recognized the voice and a smile cracked on his face.

Cassio was getting annoyed. "Seriously? Security! Remove these people so we have no more interruptions," he said into the microphone. Nevek turned around to see two guards grabbing Arys. *No!* He looked back to see Cassio giving the signal again to resume.

"No, wait!" Nevek shouted.

"That's enough, boy!" Cassio exclaimed. "Get out of here now or I'll have to remove you by force!"

Dwerth stood up and took Nevek under the arm to remove him. "Clearly, this was a bad idea," he said to himself.

"No, listen. I have been detained for housing these two," he was struggling with Dwerth as he talked. "They have been under my watch for some time now. I wish to go before these two. Take me first."

Unaware of what was going on, Arys was thrown out of the establishment, sent away with a 'get lost' from one of the guards. She panicked, wanting to know what was happening, and ran to see the 'action' on a nearby television. It was then Endy arrived on the scene. "What's going on?"

"Nothing good." Arys filled her in as they looked on.

"How's Zavier?"

Endy's tone quickly changed to a mixture of anger and annoyance. "He said he didn't want my help. He just got up and took off. Whatever."

Because of a slight delay in the broadcast, the two ladies then heard Nevek say, "Take me first."

Dwerth let go of Nevek at those words. The whole room fell silent. Urial and Jerika's eyes' both widened in disbelief. Cassio who finally broke the silence. "That crime is not punishable by death," he leaned into the microphone.

"Well, neither is what these two have been sentenced with."

"They escaped from jail," Cassio continued.

"Again, I don't believe that to be true, but what do I know? I wish to be put down first, ahead of these two. I cannot bear to see them done wrong like this."

Arys couldn't believe her ears. "Nevek, no!" she shouted at the screen.

"What is he doing?" Endy inquired, her hands over her mouth in disbelief.

"Nevek, you imbecile!" Arys shouted in anger. She had to get back inside. She looked around the immediate vicinity for a way in, but no luck. She told Endy to stay and keep watching the screen. *I can't let him do this!*

Arys came around to a corridor that looked secluded. She opened a nearby door and looked around to see if she was being watched. She was. A young, slender man walked toward her, smiling. She cocked her head, wondering why he looked familiar. *Sqett!*. She exhaled as she felt a small sense of relief. She could use his help.

The crowd started talking again. Cassio looked over at Haros and the other guards around him. No one knew what was going on in Nevek's head. Nevek wasn't even sure. He just knew he couldn't see his friends wrongfully put to death.

Officials talked with each other on stage. The commotion grew in the room. Dwerth again asked Nevek what he thought he was doing. Nevek didn't answer.

Cassio walked back onto the mic and hushed the audience. "Nevek, is it? Your form of suicide is unheard of and completely brainless. However, if it's what you'd like, we shall oblige."

The crowd cheered as Cassio told Nevek to come up onto the stage. A guard forcefully removed Jerika from the vault. She almost lost her balance, but Urial caught her. Jerika's eyes never left Nevek. The whole building focused on this young man.

Nevek and Dwerth reached the top of the stage and approached the Chancellor. Cassio met them halfway and nodded to Dwerth as if to say that he would take it from here. Dwerth looked at Nevek for a moment with confusion and walked away shaking his head.

Cassio went up to Nevek, narrow-eyed. "What are you doing, kid? Are you sure about this?"

Nevek smiled. "Hey. It's a celebration." He threw his handcuffed hands in the air. "I just want to give the people what they came to see." He put on a good act, but inside he was more nervous than he'd ever been.

Cassio gave Nevek an angered look. "Okay, smart guy,

get in there."

A guard walked him toward his destination. Nevek caught a glimpse of his friends before he looked down at the stage. He didn't want to make eye contact with them. He wasn't doing this to be seen, even though all eyes were on him. The loud roar of the crowd faded into the background. This was it. His last moments on Ceres. Of existence.

As Nevek approached the entrance of the vault, he could hear a faint "Don't do this." *Probably Jerika.* The guard took off his restraints and went to push him in, only to see him stepping in already. Nevek figured the quicker, the better. *If I'm going to die, better go ahead and get it over with.*

As the door shut, reality set in. His eyes began to water. He wasn't sure what to say or do. His mind was blank. He just sat down and crossed his legs, bowing his head so no one could see the tears running down his face.

Nevek heard the door lock and faint cheering. The box was nearly soundproof. Many people were jumping up and down, clapping and screaming. He exhaled and calmed himself, lifting his head to the door. It was going to be his focal point. A new noise began. *They've probably turned on the machine.* Only a few moments had gone by, or at least he thought so, before his vision started getting blurry. He tried to control his breathing, which grew more difficult.

Then...all went black.

CHAPTER 31

The crowd was in a frenzy. Cassio stepped to the microphone to address them. "There you have it folks. Now let's...."

The microphone cut out.

No one could hear the rest over the cheering and chatter. Cassio tapped it and looked to see what was wrong. Fearing danger, many of the guards huddled around the Chancellor, scanning the audience for trouble.

Sqett had jammed the microphone signal, allowing Arys to run up and pull the lever to get oxygen flowing again. She was quickly grabbed by one of the guards. "No! I will not let my brother do this." Sqett pushed his way to the door and opened it. Nevek had been in there over two minutes. He wasn't likely to last much longer.

"How did she get back in here?" Cassio asked aloud.

A guard ran into the vault and grabbed Sqett who had reached Nevek. The guard dragged the invader out by his garments, unaware that Sqett was still holding tightly to Nevek's motionless body.

Cassio made his way back to the podium to restore order. "Okay. Everybody, stop!" he yelled into the microphone. Nearly everyone came to a halt. Arys had broken free from one of the guards and ran over to her brother. "Time to put my nursing skills to the test," she said to herself.

"Now, what is going on here?" Cassio asked.

Sqett tried to talk under the grip of the guard who had

him in a choke hold. "Um...sir."

Cassio nodded to the guard to release him. Sqett started to cough a little as he rubbed his throat. After he gained his composure, he said, "Chancellor, if these two are being put to death for being a Christian, you will have to kill me too, because I am a Christian."

Urial, Jerika, Arys, and just about everyone else who heard it froze. "Excuse me?" Cassio inquired.

"You cannot kill these people for being Christians. It's not just."

"They escaped from prison. How many times do I have to say this?" He looked around at his guards.

"No, they didn't and I have proof," Sqett stated.

Cassio looked at him confused. "What did you say?"

Sqett felt confidence he had never felt before. He wasn't sure where it came from. He cleared his throat. "I have proof that these two did not break out of prison," he pointed to the Martians.

Cassio cocked his head. Standing by, Haros heard what was said. "He's bluffing, Cassio."

"You're bluffing," the Chancellor repeated.

"Sqett. What are you doing?" Arys whispered loudly, still tending to Nevek, who was still out. Sqett ignored her. He pulled out his slate and held it up. Cassio's eyes widened.

"Why would you presume I was bluffing if you have nothing to cover up?" Sqett asked.

Urial finally spoke up, "It's because we didn't break out of prison. He let us go."

The crowds grew silent, pondering what would happen next. Dwerth snuck up behind Sqett and grabbed his slate.

"Yeah, that's what every criminal says." He flipped the device over to Cassio.

"Hey! Give that back to me!" Sqett started to approach the Chancellor, but stopped in his tracks when Dwerth pulled out his gun.

"You mean, give you *this* back?" Cassio taunted. He dropped it on the ground and gave it one good stomp. "I'm so sorry. It slipped." He picked it up and threw it back to Sqett, who just looked at it in disbelief.

Some parts of the room filled with chatter, questioning what had happened to the Chancellor they thought they knew. Others started making their way out when they saw Dwerth draw his gun.

"Chancellor, we need to stay on task," Haros said.

"Yes. Let the festivities continue," Cassio announced.

"No! You cannot do this!" Sqett shouted.

Cassio was fed up at this point. "Guards! Detain this nuisance!" he yelled at he started to walk away.

His guardsman grabbed Sqett and forced him to the ground. They put his hands behind his back. Dwerth holstered his gun and came up to put restraints on him, as many that remained starting cheering again.

Arys looked around in fear, scared to say anything. She just held her brother.

"What about the girl?" another guard asked Cassio.

After thinking for a second, "Nah, leave her."

The cheering escalated now that there were no more interruptions. Back to what everyone came to see. Two criminals put to death. One guard grabbed Jerika again and walked her to the vault. She tried to put up a fight, but it was no use as the guard was much bigger.

"Chancellor, you cannot do this!" Urial shouted. "Let us go!" It was no use. Cassio had already walked off the platform, and the noise made it very unlikely that Urial's voice was heard anyway.

Salem had made his way to the building. He came up to Endy who was standing outside, nervously watching a television. "Some event, huh?"

"Yeah, my friends have been wrongfully sentenced."

"Your friends? You know them too?"

Endy looked at him funny. "Yeah, do you?"

Salem let out a little laugh. "Some of them, yes. I only know them through someone I met recently. I gotta get in there though."

"Good luck. My friend was in there and got kicked out. She had to sneak back in there."

"You think you could get me in? I've gotta do the right thing."

Endy stared at Salem with an odd look. She felt as if she knew him. It was a strange feeling. They got so lost in their conversation that they weren't paying attention to the monitor. That's when they heard a gunshot. They both looked up at the monitor in awe. All they saw was Haros with his gun drawn. *Who did he shoot at?*

The crowd was in a frenzy as people started screaming and running for the doors. Some were getting trampled as they were pushing their way out. Salem grabbed Endy and pressed against a wall to avoid the stampede. They stood there waiting until there was an opening.

"These two are going to die today even if I have to do

it!" Chief Haros shouted. His shot, meant for Jerika, hit the guard that was wrestling with her. The loud *bang* woke Nevek up as well. He struggled to breathe a little but Arys was able to calm him down. A couple of the guards quickly tended to their injured comrade.

"Chief, what are you doing?" Cassio asked as he came back onto the platform.

"Chancellor, we've had too many interruptions," Haros said, as members of Cassio's service men started to surround him with their guns drawn as well. Haros' rage was growing by the minute as the last of the crowd emptied.

"Haros, drop your gun." Cassio said calmly as he slowly approached him.

"No!" he shouted as he put his hand up as if to say 'stay back.' "You don't know how long I've waited for this day. Someone recently reminded me what happened when we were young. When I was young. A lot of people lost their lives to start this planet—my mother and sister among them. Now, tell your men to get out of my way so I can finish what we came here for."

Cassio didn't know what to say. There was a moment of silence. Haros still had his gun pointed towards Jerika when a voice broke the silence.

"Chief, don't do it."

The voice startled Haros and a couple of guards as they pointed their guns towards where sound was coming from. Salem walked in from a side door with his hands raised. Endy came in behind him and stayed out of firing range. Nevek began to be coherent

"And who are you?" Haros asked.

"My name is Salem. I'm an educator over in Valtux.

I've been watching what's been going on and I'm concerned that what we're doing isn't right."

What's he doing here? Nevek thought as he cracked a smile.

"Chief, don't shoot. I'm here to tell you that you guys are making a big mistake. Chancellor, do not kill these two. They come in peace."

Jerika spoke quickly after, "That's what we've been telling you. You let us go. We mean you no harm."

Haros looked at Cassio. "They're just messing with your mind, Cassio. Trying to get into your head."

Cassio stood, not knowing what to do. Seeing the opportunity however, Salem continued, "Chancellor, if you do this, it could end up starting a war between our planets. I think I could speak for everyone here when I say that that is something nobody wants."

Haros grew angrier the more they stalled. He still had his gun aimed at Salem, and Cassio's men had theirs aimed at him. His eyes nervously darted back and forth between Salem, the Chancellor, the guns, and the prisoners.

Nevek stood up, keeping in mind the dream he had while he was unconscious. "There's no way these Martians did what you say they did. You don't know them like I do. If they say they were let go, I believe them."

Sqett chimed in. "Mr. Salem has a point. Others would not think highly of us if you go through with this. They would decimate us, even to the annihilation of this planet."

"Don't listen to them! These people killed my family!" Haros shouted.

"No! No, it wasn't them. These two do not represent the Christians that banned us. They weren't even born yet,"

Salem reasoned.

"He's right." Urial finally added to the mix. "They were of a different sect of Christians who had no right to do what they did."

Cassio was confused. "Different sect? How do you know all of this? It was classified information."

Salem spoke again, "I am one of the few survivors of the people who first came here from Mars. I saw what happened. I lived though the horror of the banishment. What my parents and I went through…my family and friends…I lost people that I loved too." He shook his head, remembering the sadness of those times. "Those people called themselves 'The Soldiers of Christ.' They were heavily influenced by a government that was trying to convert people by force, and in doing so, misinterpreting passages from the Bible. And even though I lost a lot at the hands of The Soldiers of Christ, I do have to thank them. Because of them, I actually became a Christian. I wanted to know why they did what they did. To get inside their heads. And what I found was that they were wrong. And these two right here, they weren't a part of that. These are different Christians—*true* Christians," Salem explained as he pointed to Urial and Jerika.

Cassio felt sorry after hearing the truth, but was still confused. "But aren't all Christians the same?"

"They are to me!" Haros said as he fanned his weapon across the room and landed on Urial. Time seemed to go in slow motion.

"No!" a few people shouted.

BANG!

CHAPTER 32

*B*ang! Another shot. Haros grabbed his chest and fell hard to the ground. Arys seemed to be the only one interested in seeing where Haros' bullet went.

"Nevek!" Everyone turned to see Nevek laying on the floor.

Urial just stared at him. "He...he just jumped in front of me," Urial said.

Arys reached her brother first, and Sqett, Endy, Salem, and Jerika rushed over to aid however they could. Cassio went to see Haros with Dwerth and some of his men.

"Nevek, can you hear me?" Arys asked as she turned him over.

Nevek let out a scream and grabbed his side. He let out a deep breath. "So that's what it's like to get shot."

"Endy, we have to get him to a hospital. Call an ambulance," Arys commanded.

"Is he going to be okay?" Urial asked from afar.

"I don't know," Arys answered. "That was incredibly stupid, kiddo," she scolded her brother.

"But it was very brave," Salem added. "What made you do it?"

Trying to hold in his pain, Nevek said, "I don't know really. I didn't want to see Urial die on his only trip to this planet. Ahh!"

"You are quite insane, Nevek," Sqett exclaimed.

"I just felt I had to... from this dream I had while I was out. It gave me a peace I never felt before."

"What did you see?" Jerika inquired.

"Well, there was white all around me. And there was this person with wings."

"Like an angel?" Salem interrupted.

"Sure. Is that...er...what their called?" Nevek groaned as Arys applied pressure to the wound.

"Yeah."

"Well, it was just me and this...angel...and he told me not to worry. Jesus would be with me."

Jerika started to tear up as she put her hands over her mouth in awe. Salem smiled as he sat down.

"You encountered Jesus?" Sqett asked.

"That's weird," Arys said.

"No. Just the angel," explained Nevek.

"He's dead," they heard abruptly from across the room. Dwerth was kneeling over Haros' body. Everyone was in shock. The women covered their mouths. Cassio turned away from the corpse on the floor. "Get him out of here," he commanded his men. He then looked across the room. "And you!" Cassio snarled at Urial. "Er, get him out of those." He was disgusted at the turn of events. Dwerth walked over, never taking his eyes off of the prisoner. Urial was nervous, certain he was going to be harmed. Dwerth took the restraints off without saying a word, and walked away to help some of the guards with Haros' corpse.

"I want you two to board your ships and leave and never return to this planet," he said to the Martians, who nodded. He was upset, but more shocked at everything that happened, so he tried to remain calm. He turned his attention to the Cereans. "As for the rest of you, I hearby ban Christianity on Ceres. Anyone caught teaching this, will be terminated. Especially you, Salem. In fact, consider yourself fired. I trust you all to see yourself out," he said as he turned around and walked out.

Everyone stared in shock. Sqett started to say something but was stopped by Salem, who held his hand up as if to say *It's not worth it.*

Medics arrived, and Dwerth showed them where help was needed. He followed Cassio out, leaving a few guards to haul off the corpse.

As they walked out, Dwerth leaned over to Cassio, "You're not gonna see if they leave?"

"They'll leave if they know what's good for them."

The medics walked over and looked at Nevek's wound. He winced in pain when they touched it. The bullet had gone right through him, so he was losing a lot of blood. Arys kept pressure on the wound, and the rest of the friends stayed gathered around him. The medics made them move out of the way and told Arys they would handle it from there. She didn't want to leave his side, but knew it had to be done.

The group of friends looked on helplessly, not really understanding the medical jargon being used. They just knew that their friend was not in good shape.

One medic applied gauze, but Nevek had bled through it in no time. "We're going to have to cauterize the hole," one said to the other. There was no time to numb the area. They had to act fast.

"This is gonna hurt, kid," one of them said. "But we gotta close it up."

"Just do it!" he yelled.

The other medic brought the equipment over and set it

up. Nevek had bled through another patch of gauze. The lead medic pulled it away and touched Nevek's wound with the hot tool. Nevek howled in agony, and it resounded throughout the whole building. Endy had to look away. They turned Nevek over to do the other side.

"Don't move, or we can't get it," the medic said, trying to calm him down. Nevek fought every impulse to move, to twist away from the pain as they burned the wound close. It felt like it would never end.

The medics finished and began packing up their equipment. "You're gonna be just fine, kid," one of them said as they patted his back.

Arys ran to his side. "I still can't believe you did that. What were you thinking?" Arys asked as she hugged her brother.

"Eh, I have a nurse for a sister," Nevek chuckled, trying to lighten the mood as he bottled up his pain.

"Well, thank you, friend," Urial said as he put a hand on Nevek's shoulder.

"Yes, and it was that kind of love that Jesus showed each and every one of us," Salem added. "No man has greater love than this: that he lays down his life for his friends."

"Yes, that's true."

"Oh, my apologies. My name is Salem Yusek. Very nice to meet you both," he said as he shook the Martians hands.

"Yes, and thank you too," Jerika said with dried tears in her eyes. "If it wasn't for you, I'd be dead."

"Yeah, don't mention it. Just trying to help out fellow believers."

"Hey, how did you know we're not from the sect that banished those to this planet?"

"Well, I didn't, but I do now," Salem laughed. "So, what sect are you from anyway?"

"No sect, sir," Urial answered. "Just part of the assembly of Christ."

Salem extended his hand again. "Pleasure to meet you brethren. Me too." Urial and Jerika looked at each other and smiled.

Feeling as if he needed to say something, Sqett interjected. "Well, I am going to miss you two."

"Yeah, we'll miss you guys too," Jerika said as she choked up again.

Arys picked up her brother. "Well, let's go back to my pod so we can officially say goodbye. I'm sure you guys are hungry and Nevek should get some rest."

"I thought your chancellor told us to leave?"

"Eh, what he doesn't know won't hurt him."

CHAPTER 33

I t had been a crazy ride. Everyone was exhausted. No one wanted it to end this way, but they all admitted that they were glad it was ending. They weren't sure how much more they could take.

They laughed, recalling how they thought Urial was a stalker. But, other parts of the past several sols weren't so humorous. Arys and Nevek were now fatherless. And their grandfather would probably never speak to them again.

But the group focused most on the good memories they would remember from their adventures. How they met. The friends they've made. Endy showing Jerika around. And there was Sqett's conversion to Christianity. He told them how Salem helped him to see the truth. All of it made them feel good inside. The walk down memory lane continued all the way back to Arys' pod and continued as they sat inside.

No one wanted to cook anything. Half of them weren't even hungry in the first place. Most of them just wanted to sleep. It had been a physically and emotionally draining past few sols. It was nice to just kick back and relax.

Urial and Jerika did eat a bit to fuel them for the long trip ahead of them. After Urial was done eating, Nevek asked, "How do you not fall asleep in that ship on such a long trip?"

"Oh, there's an autopilot. I can sleep whenever I want." A couple of them laughed. "And this time, I'll have another pilot with me," he pointed to Jerika.

"Oh, that's right. I forgot. Well again, we're gonna miss you. I'm glad to have met you both."

Arys agreed. "Yes. Thank you for teaching us that there's more out there than just our planet. You guys are wonderful."

"Yes, do come again," Sqett blurted out. "Oh, wait…"

It was an awkward moment, but everyone was in such a joyful spirit, they just laughed it off.

"I think what he means is, it was good to have met you both," Nevek said as he stood up, holding his side.

"Yes, and we're forever grateful for saving our lives. Thank you again," Urial said.

"I still can't believe you jumped in front of that bullet," Arys said, shaking her head.

"Hey, I'm sure they would have done the same thing for us. I was just trying to do the right thing," Nevek explained. Everyone agreed.

As Salem sat there, Nevek's words struck a chord. "That reminds me," he started. He leaned over to them. "You said you wanted to do the right thing. Right by whom?"

They were puzzled. No one answered. Not even the Martians knew where Salem was going with it.

"I don't think I understand," Nevek spoke on behalf of everyone.

Salem got up off his seat now. "You said the *right* thing. As opposed to the *wrong* thing. But how do we determine that? What makes something good or right and other things wrong or bad?"

"Uh, well…I don't know. I guess I never really thought about it. Why?"

Salem went on to explain, "See, morals are one of the best proofs that God exists. Christians live by a standard, and that's *God's* standard. He is the ruler of the universe, so he makes the rules. People who don't believe there is a God can't say the same thing. Well, that is they're living inconsistent lives."

"What do you mean?" Arys inquired.

"If there is no God, there wouldn't be morals. No one could say anything is right or wrong. Everyone would just live however they wanted. But inside each of us is the image of God. He's put inside each one of us this moral compass. We all believe the same things to be good and bad. And we strive to live according to his rules, whether we believe in them or not. Those who don't believe in him are inconsistent because they're not living according to their worldview, which would be chaos."

"But, they're not. They're still living according to the morals of God," Urial added, beginning to understand where Salem was heading.

It was becoming clearer to Nevek too. What Salem said moved him. This brought his mind back to his dream of the angel. *What did it mean? Jesus was with me?*

"That's brilliant, Mr. Yusek!" Urial exclaimed.

"Yeah, I had never thought of that before," Jerika said. "You know, if you ever feel the need to keep teaching, you could always come back to Mars."

"Well, thank you, but I think my place is still here. I might be too old to make that trip anyway," he chuckled.

Everyone started conversing and saying their goodbyes, except for Nevek. Thoughts flooded his head. It was as if everything he learned about God struck him all at once. To the rest in the room, he just had a blank stare on his face.

He finally snapped out of it and looked up at everyone he had met since this little escapade started. Since Jerika arrived and taught him about God. They were all in one room, together. Salem, Endy, Sqett, Jerika, and Urial. He appreciated getting to know them. So much so that he unknowingly cracked a smile.

Arys noticed her brother zoned out next to her. She nudged his shoulder. "Hey. You okay?"

It hit him like a smack in the face. His eyes almost popped out of his face as he cursed out loud. Everyone stopped and looked at him.

"Woah! Was that necessary?" Arys asked.

Nevek looked at Jerika with big eyes. "I want to become a Christian."

Everyone was baffled. A couple of them weren't even sure what Nevek said.

"What did you say?" Salem asked.

"How do I become a Christian?" Nevek responded.

"I thought that's what you said." Jerika said. "Are you sure you want to? What made you change your mind?"

Nevek stood up. "It was everything you guys have said, but the dream sealed it."

Jerika was excited about what she was hearing. She had come all this way to tell others about Christ, not knowing what would happen. She wasn't even expecting even one person to respond, but now *two*? God was doing wonders on Ceres.

Nevek continued, "That angel said that Jesus was with me. I didn't know what that meant until now, seeing you all here."

"Oh, snap!" Arys interrupted. "I don't believe it!"

Nevek turned around to his sister. "You see it too?"

"What do you see?" Urial questioned.

Arys' eyes were opened wide. Her jaw dropped as she cupped her mouth. "All of you here. The first letters of all your names. Jerika, Endy, Sqett, Urial, Salem... They spell out JESUS."

It took a second for everyone to realize it. Some smiled, and a few more jaws succumbed to gravity.

"That could just be a coincidence though, no?" Sqett pondered out loud.

"I don't think it is," Nevek claimed. "Teach me."

"You sure you want to? It's a big responsibility." Salem explained.

"I can handle it. What do I have to do?"

"Well, do you believe that Jesus is the Son of God, who came down to die so that we could be forgiven of your sins?" Salem asked.

"Yes, I do," Nevek confessed.

"Then let's wash away your sins."

Salem explained from the Bible that the way people entered into Christianity was through baptism. It was the rite in which one is immersed in water to contact the blood of Christ, which ultimately forgives their transgressions. After then, a person was restored back as a child of God.

Salem filled Arys' bathtub with water. He was advanced in age, so he gave the honors to Urial to baptize Nevek. It would be his first one, so he was a little nervous.

"That makes two of us," Nevek replied. "So, what now?"

"Well, this cleanses your soul of any sins you have, never to be a burden to you again."

"Got it. So you're gonna dunk me in this water."

"Exactly." Urial further explained what it all entailed and they were both ready to go. Nevek stepped into the tub, sat down, and held his nose to not get water up it. Urial took him under his back and eased Nevek under the water.

Water clogged Nevek's ears as he kept his eyes closed. When he came up, he felt like a different person. The water rushed off his body as he arose. He felt refreshed. A feeling entirely new to him, but he liked it. As he stood up, Urial told him he had just been baptized in the name of Jesus. Sqett and Jerika applauded. Salem asked him how he felt. "Like a new man," Nevek replied with a smile.

"God was really working on your heart," Jerika said.

"Yeah, I guess he was."

"I want to be baptized too," Endy stated almost out of nowhere.

Jerika turned to her. "Are you sure?"

"Yes, I believe that Jesus died for me. I want him to take away my evil too."

Jerika was elated. She thought she was dreaming. God was awesome. He had worked out things for his glory, and Jerika was thrilled to be able to be a part of it.

"Well, get in here," Urial motioned her into the tub as he helped Nevek out. "I now baptize you in the name of our Lord Jesus," he said as he plunged her under. She came up also feeling restored. She started to cry as she got out and was greeted with a hug from Nevek.

"What about you, Arys?" Urial asked.

"Um, no thanks. I think I'll pass."

The next few moments were a blur of hugs, smiles, and well wishes. The two that were wet dried off, and the others said their final goodbyes. The Martians were thanked as they headed out the door. Salem and Sqett had to get home too, so they followed suit. It was just Arys, Nevek, and Endy that remained.

They all were more exhausted than before. Arys suggested that Endy and Nevek just sleep at her place, to which they agreed. Endy went into the bathroom for a moment, leaving Arys and Nevek out in the living area. Nevek laid down on the sofa as Arys came up from behind.

"So, what are you going to do now?" she asked him.

"I don't know," he replied. His body was tired, but the question reverberated in his mind as he closed his eyes. What was he going to do? Should he finish school? He already missed a few classes. And he wasn't sure what career to choose. Maybe Salem could teach him some things. He was getting old though. How much longer would he be able to teach him? What about Mars? He could really learn a lot from his new friends. They were leaving though. He most likely would never see them again. What about Arys? Could she help? Too many scenarios played out, but all of a sudden, he knew what he had to do. He opened his eyes, got on his feet and walked towards the door.

"Where are you going?" he heard Arys ask.

Endy returned to see Nevek at the opened door.

"I have to go with them," Nevek replied.

Arys chuckled. "With who? Urial and Jerika?"

"Yeah. I have to go to Mars."

"Are you're serious?" Endy asked, her head cocked.

"I wanna learn more about this new life...and the only

way to do that is to go to Mars."

Arys started laughing nervously. "You can't just go with them. They probably don't even have room for you."

"Urial's ship looks big enough. I saw it earlier."

"But everything you have is here. Your family. Your friends. Your school…"

"Right. School?" Nevek interrupted. "I haven't been to class in sols. I already missed the final. There's nothing for me to learn here. I can get a better education on Mars."

After remaining quiet, Endy finally spoke up. "Did you lose some brain cells when you blacked out? I think the vault made you crazy." She tried not to sound humorous.

Nevek threw his hands up in frustration. He began pressing his temples. "Guys, I'm not crazy! Okay?" He looked at his sister. "Arys, do you remember what dad used to say? Don't follow others. Make your own path. This is me making my path. Sorry, but I have to go. I need to find more."

Arys and Endy could only watch as Nevek turned around and opened the door. He walked down the hall and descended the stairs to the lobby. He ran out the main door to the road, hoping he didn't miss his flight to Mars. He looked left, but didn't see anyone. He looked right and saw his friends off in the distance. With as much energy as he could, he ran after them.

"Guys, hold up!" he shouted.

They both turned around. Jerika squinted her eyes. "Nevek? Is everything okay?"

He stopped in front of them, almost out of breath. "I'm going with you."

THE END

EPILOGUE

Even after pleading with the Zand police department, Talbot was not able to get his job back. Dwerth, however, was able to refer him to the force in Valtux. It was a different squadron, but Talbot was grateful to at least have his old job back. He was disappointed at not making on the planetary force, but decided maybe it wasn't for him. He was also grateful that he didn't have to deal with big affairs anymore like the one that recently took place. He hoped things would get back to the way they used to be.

That didn't quite go over well, as he had to bust Zavier for disturbing the peace. Zavier was trying to drink his sorrows away and became belligerent with a taproom employee. He was going to be locked up for a while.

Presently, things were a quieter for Talbot. He had just gotten a call from a woman who said her child had found something strange. After everything that recently went on, he really wasn't that surprised, but was sure it was just going to be something mundane. He'd gotten those calls before. Even though the planet wasn't that old, people were always discovering new things.

Talbot pulled up to a house to find three boys sitting on a curb. One of them was holding something. He got out and smelled a foul odor coming from the boys. Talbot had to hold his arm to his nose for a second. As he neared them, he looked at their faces, one of which looked familiar, but he couldn't place it.

"I heard you found something, boys," he said, to start the conversation.

"Yeah, this," the boy with the treasure said. He got up and gave it to the officer. Talbot quickly realized the sour stench was coming from him.

"Woah! Were you boys playing in garbage?" He didn't mean to be so straightforward, but he didn't have a choice. He took whatever it was from the boy and started inspecting it.

One of the other boys got up, "Yeah. We dared him to go into in the sewer." He laughed.

Talbot looked up at the familiar boy. Seeing him up close, it started to bother him. "Have we met before?" he asked the lad, while still looking at what appeared to be a netbook.

"Yeah. I was the one who showed you those spaceships."

That's why I recognize him. "Oh, yeah. Thanks again," he saluted. "Sorry. What was your name again?"

"Kennon," he replied.

"Kennon, thanks."

"Are they okay?"

"Is who okay?"

"Those people that crashed here."

"Oh, I don't really know what happened to them."

Kennon looked sad. "I hope they're okay."

"I'm sure they are," Talbot tried to reassure him. "So, tell me about this you found. What is it?"

"I don't know. My mom freaks out over the littlest things. I guess that's why she called you."

"Well, she was just doing the right thing," he smiled.

He hadn't seen anything like it before. He tried to clean the rest of the sewage off of it to get a better look. He finally got it clean enough that he could make out its faded, yellow casing.

"Did you guys touch this at all?" he asked the boys.

Kennon answered, "No."

"Okay, well, I'm just going to take this with me. It doesn't look like it works, but thanks for letting me know about it," he said as he held it up to them. "And, no more playing in the sewers, please?"

They agreed, and Kennon and his friends went back into the house. Talbot snickered as heard the mother yell, "Good grief, you stink! I told you to stay outside!"

He inspected the device all the way back to his car. It looked similar to his slate. After he got in, he saw what looked like a button on the back, so he pressed it and it turned on. He flipped it over and saw a cross as a loading screen. It then went to a table of contents. Naturally, he picked the first chapter, 'Genesis,' and started reading.

"In the beginning,
God created the heavens and the earth..."

Kevin Micuch
is a combination author/entrepreneur/Christian whose two
kids keep him and his wife busy in their home near
Tampa, Florida.

He can be reached at
Knives822@gmail.com

or @k_mychuk
on Twitter and Instagram

74129470R00128

Made in the USA
Columbia, SC
10 September 2019